DROW NIGHTRUNNER

DROW NIGHTRUNNER

CHRONICLES OF SHADOW BOURNE™

BOOK SEVEN

MARTHA CARR

MICHAEL ANDERLE

LMBPN

DISRUPTIVE IMAGINATION

This book is a work of fiction. All of the characters, organizations, and events portrayed in this novel are either products of the author's imagination or are used fictitiously. Sometimes both.

Cover by Fantasy Book Design

A Michael Anderle Production

LMBPN Publishing
2375 E. Tropicana Avenue, Suite 8-305
Las Vegas, Nevada 89119 USA

Version 1.00, July 2024
ebook ISBN: 979-8-88878-258-3
Print ISBN: 979-8-88878-991-9

THE DROW NIGHTRUNNER TEAM

Thanks to our JIT Readers

Christopher Gilliard
Dorothy Lloyd
Jan Hunnicutt

Editor

SkyFyre Editing Team

CHAPTER ONE

Ellis shivered. Normally, she didn't mind the cold, but she'd been on the rubber Zodiac for an hour in the dark in drenched clothing, continuously sprayed by waves. Salt had crusted on her skin, and the constant bobbing nauseated her. Thoughts of Charlie surfaced in her mind, and she didn't have the energy to push them down. The numb exhaustion made it harder to wrap her mind around the identity of her rescuer. Sebastian had introduced himself as not only a half-drow but also her cousin.

As Sebastian removed his ski mask, the other five soldiers on the Zodiac did the same. The group was a mix of men and women. Some were clearly half-drow like Ellis and Sebastian, and some appeared to be fully human.

Ellis stuffed her hands in her pockets for warmth as much as anything else. The test tube Claire had given her nestled deep in the fabric. It held the phage serum that would cure her father, along with Ilva and Ulivi. Her cold feet restlessly tapped the rubber boat's floor. She couldn't ask them to stop pulling survivors out of the water, but after they had wrapped up their rescue operations, she would have to find a way to get to shore.

Ellis had a million questions, but Sebastian waved them away, too busy pulling people out of the water. He promised there would be time later. Now, he sat at the prow, eyes on the burning wreckage of Marusya Klimova's yacht. At the wheel, a petite woman with red hair and pale blue skin steered around a wedge of burning metal bobbing in the sea.

Ellis enjoyed the brief burst of warmth as the Zodiac puttered by. Her vision blurred with exhaustion, distorted by the flames, but she thought she saw something familiar floating in the distance behind it: strands of blonde hair swirling on the surface like seagrass.

"*Over there!*" Ellis screamed, pointing.

The woman at the wheel looked at Sebastian for confirmation. At his nod, the Zodiac's engine sputtered, and the raft slowly turned. Ellis urged it to go faster, but they were in a field of sharp debris, and Ellis had no desire to go back into the drink. She hoped her eyes hadn't been playing tricks on her. As they approached, it became apparent that she had seen true. It was Claire, all right—floating face-down in the water.

"I've got her!" Sebastian cried, hauling Claire into the boat by her life jacket. It was all Ellis could do not to wrest her mother from his hands.

Ellis stood up to elbow her way to the front of the boat, but strong hands pushed her down. Another of the black-clad soldiers moved forward, a medical kit in his hands.

"She's not breathing," Sebastian whispered, and Ellis held her breath in solidarity.

The medic leaned over Claire and placed a hand on her chest. He then pulled a small plastic tube out of the med kit. "I'm going to clear the water in her lungs." Ellis assumed he was going to use a human medical device, but the fingers of the medic's left hand curled as he positioned the tube.

He's using shadow magic.

It wasn't drow medicine—or human medicine, for that matter. It was something between the two. Ellis' mind was blank, but a remote part thought Trissa would really like to see this. Ellis' field of vision narrowed, and all she could see was her mother's pale, wet face streaked with hanks of blond hair.

After an interminable moment, she coughed. Relief flooded through Ellis' body.

"We've got to get her to the med bay," the medic said, which incited a brief disagreement.

Sebastian wanted to look for more survivors in the wreckage. The medic wanted to take Claire...where? Where had the Zodiac come from? The sea surrounding the wreckage was velvety black, and the burning wreckage made it impossible for Ellis' eyes to adjust to the darkness. There was at least one other Zodiac circling the yacht, looking for survivors.

"The chance of finding more survivors is slim, and the *Daytripper* is still looking. If we don't get this woman back to the *Eel* in the next twenty minutes, she's probably going to die."

Ellis blinked rapidly. Before she could consciously think about what she was doing, she reached over the side of the Zodiac and swiped a splintered board from the water.

"Do what the medic says, or I will put a hole in this raft." Ellis' voice shook.

Sebastian's eyebrows went skyward. The expression gave Ellis déjà vu, but she had no time to explore why.

"Then the raft would sink, and she'd get hypothermic." He nodded at Claire. "And Jerel wouldn't be able to help her since he would also be in the water." He indicated the medic, whose face was grim.

"Please," Ellis pleaded.

Sebastian surveyed the burning wreckage and sighed. "All right. Take us back to the *Eel*."

The Zodiac puttered free of the wreckage in minutes. With the eerie bobbing fires at her back, Ellis' eyes began to adjust. They headed out in a straight line, but the horizon was still a flat black line between the ocean and the sky.

Ellis shivered and frowned. The air got colder, and the Zodiac puttered to a stop. Sebastian stood up, feet planted in a wide stance. "I'll open the gate." Goosebumps rose on Ellis' arms, and a chill spread into her bones. *What gate?*

Her cousin—assuming that Sebastian had been telling the truth about that—raised his hands and drew a sigil in the air. Ellis felt briefly furious at her own lack of shadow magic. A moment later, an archway appeared in the air, and she understood what Sebastian was doing. The edges of the archway glittered and twisted, light stretching oddly at the verges. It was like a window in the sky, opening onto a different reality.

A reality wherein a massive ship was floating twenty feet away.

Ellis now understood why she was cold. Someone had cloaked an entire ship with an invisibility spell. Not a small one, either. The sleek craft in front of Ellis was at least five hundred feet long, with the lowest deck four stories above the water. In contrast to Klimova's yacht, this ship had military lines. *No swimming pools here.* The scale of the invisibility spell was astonishing. How many shadow mages had it taken? The drow in the Homestead might have been able to manage this if fifty of them had worked together at the same time. Sebastian was looking at her with a bemused expression.

"Cool, huh?" he asked.

Ellis gulped and nodded. "How do you do it?"

The Zodiac moved toward the side of the boat, and he shook his head. "Later."

Someone lowered a small platform from the side of the ship until it was just below the water. The woman at the wheel moved the Zodiac on top of that platform with great precision. All the soldiers except Jerel sprang into action, clipping carabiners to loops on the Zodiac's side.

"Try not to fall off," Sebastian suggested as they lurched out of the water.

The swaying of the ropes and bobbing of the ship set off another wave of nausea, and Ellis puked over the side. It was a waste of the granola bar one of the soldiers had given her half an hour ago, but she couldn't stop herself. The ship she stepped onto a minute later was very well-maintained, so she doubted they were short on supplies.

Ellis marveled at the dozens of humans and drow

working together to get them off the Zodiac. Sebastian and the others stripped off their wet clothes and dressed in uniforms brought by other crew members. Four of the sailors—the ones who looked fully human—peeled thick wetsuits off their bodies, talking in low, cheerful voices.

Ellis held Claire's hand until two medics approached with a stretcher and carefully loaded her mother onto it. "You've got to let go," Jerel said, keeping two fingers on Claire's pulse. Ellis did, and Jerel led the medics toward a hatch into the interior of the ship. Ellis started to follow them, but Sebastian put a hand on her arm. "There's nothing you can do. And my people are the best in the world."

"What is this?" Ellis asked. She had a thousand questions, but somehow, that was the only one she could pick from the barrel.

Sebastian grinned, and his purple freckles flashed a richer color. He swept his hands around to take in the operation. "This, cousin, is the *Violet Eel.* Welcome aboard!"

"I need to see your captain," Ellis said, hand wrapping back around the test tube in her pocket.

"That would be me," Sebastian replied.

Just then, the ship surged up, cresting a swell, and Ellis' stomach went with it. She sprinted to the railing, but nothing came up. The sea had already commandeered the entirety of her stomach contents. When she managed to straighten, Sebastian was standing next to her, clapping her on the back.

"Seasick?" he asked. When she nodded, he reached into a pocket and pulled out a crinkly plastic bag with a cheerful orange design. He fished out a wrapped candy and handed it to her.

"Ginger chews. I buy 'em in Tokyo. Best thing in the world for seasickness."

Ellis chewed dubiously, thinking she might puke the second it hit her stomach, but the sweet candy seemed to calm it. After she swallowed the first one, Sebastian handed her another. When she was done, Ellis said the first thing that came to mind.

"If you're the captain, how come *you* have to eat candy for seasickness?" she asked, feeling miserable.

Sebastian grinned. "Bad luck."

Ellis tried to focus on the horizon rather than the waves lapping at the ship. "I don't even know how to swim."

Sebastian didn't seem surprised. "Most drow can't. Not at first. Not a lot of pools in their caves." He tossed her the bag of ginger candies. "Keep this. You'll need it."

Ellis nodded eagerly. "I will. The Zodiacs are pretty bumpy, and I need one of your sailors to take me to shore."

The amusement on his face was infuriating. He wasn't taking her seriously. "I can't do that. We're still running search and rescue. I realize that not everyone on that yacht was a shining example of humanity, but we'll save them if we can. Besides, they might have useful information."

"You don't understand." Her fingers tightened around the test tube. "It's urgent."

"Is someone going to die if it doesn't happen in the next twenty-four hours?" Sebastian asked.

"Maybe." She was so distraught that Sebastian's eyes narrowed. "My mother was working on a cure for one of Marusya Klimova's diseases. My father is very sick. He's your uncle if you've been telling the truth about us being cousins." She held the test tube out. She would have to trust him.

Sebastian's eyes grew stormy. "Your mother was working on a bioweapon with Marusya Klimova."

"That was the cover story, or at least, it was a separate project," Ellis argued. The ginger candies had kickstarted her appetite, and now she was nauseated *and* starving, as well as light-headed. She didn't have time to explain the intricacies of Claire Burton's betrayals. *An immortal god wouldn't have time for that,* she thought wryly.

"So, one of your mother's projects was an attempt to kill everyone on Earth, and the other one was a cure for a mysterious disease?"

"Yes." Ellis was desperate. She had to believe the cure was real since she had to believe her father would live.

Sebastian looked at the test tube, spinning it between his fingers. "I'll have my science team take a look at this. If they assure me it's not a civilization-ending bug, then... well, we'll see."

Ellis wanted to argue more, but Sebastian had made up his mind. His jaw was set and his mind had moved on to other things.

She couldn't swim to shore. And even if she could get one of the Zodiacs into the water, she wasn't sure she could drive it. She would play along for now, and if she needed to, she would make a move.

Sebastian ushered Ellis along the deck. They passed a second Zodiac, whose crew of six was unloading the raft's contents onto the deck. They had laid out three bodies.

Ellis, who knew they were dead the minute she saw them, veered toward them with trepidation.

"Are you sure you want to look?" Sebastian asked.

"I have to," Ellis said. She went to the smallest body first.

It was Marusya Klimova.

She looked smaller than Ellis remembered, shoeless and bedraggled. The world-killing anger that had animated her was gone, leaving skin and bones in its wake. For the first time, she looked like she was at peace.

Ellis felt a little of that peace at the knowledge that Marusya was dead. The woman had been dangerous, and that danger was now over. Guilty relief flooded up Ellis' spine, and she turned her attention to the two other bodies. One was a Russian guard. The other was Gaspar. Ellis felt a stab of regret when she looked at his face, the same color as the ocean. She hadn't agreed with his choices, but he'd thought he was doing the right thing for his people.

A second stretcher came onto the deck, and the black-clad soldiers loaded a small figure onto it. Ellis rushed over to see a wide-eyed Mirelle being carried away.

"You should put a guard on her," Ellis told Sebastian, who had joined her at the second Zodiac. "Do you have lightsilk? She could be dangerous."

"We've got all the toys," Sebastian said, his face grim. "We've been surveilling that yacht for weeks. Why do you think we torpedoed it?"

Ellis put the pieces together. She remembered the dark shape she'd seen in the water an instant before the yacht exploded. Apparently, it had come from this ship. It was not like there was anyone else around. In light of this new information, Sebastian's shining armor looked rusty. She resolved not to trust him yet. "There were a lot of innocent people on that yacht. How did you know which ones you'd kill?"

She asked loudly, and a few of the soldiers unloading the Zodiac gave her the side-eye.

"We didn't," Sebastian replied. "But her project was very dangerous. We couldn't let it continue."

"There was a drow woman on the boat. Her name was Lola. I need to know if you found her," Ellis said.

"She was one of the drow separatists working with Marusya?"

Ellis absorbed his question. It meant Sebastian knew quite a bit about what had been happening on the yacht. The *Violet Eel* hadn't just been looking at Marusya's yacht through a telescope. The ship had been listening to their conversations. Considering the cloaking technology Ellis had seen, it was even possible they'd had spies aboard.

"Lola was the leader of the separatist group. She had bright purple skin and pale lilac hair. Very distinctive."

Sebastian nodded and pulled a handheld radio from his belt. He relayed Ellis' description and waited. The soldier on the other end said that none of the rescue boats had pulled anyone matching that description out of the water.

"You have to send your people out again. If there was any chance she escaped…"

Sebastian glanced in the direction of the wreckage, which was just an orange glow on the horizon. The implication was clear. If Lola was out there, she was probably dead.

"Hey, Val!" Sebastian called. A muscular woman with clipped red hair looked up from where she was coiling rope on the deck. She seemed to be in her late thirties or early forties, and her arms were covered in nautical tattoos. As she walked over to Sebastian, she eyed Ellis with open distrust. "Are you up for going out again?" Sebastian asked. He relayed what Ellis had told him about Lola.

"You think it's worth it?" Val asked, eyeing the burning wreckage.

"No, but I'm trying to make a good impression on my cousin," Sebastian told her. Ellis snorted. He apparently didn't rule his ship with an iron fist.

Val's wetsuit was in a pile on the deck. It did not look enticing, but she sighed and nodded. "We'll keep an eye out for anyone who is especially purple. And I get your dessert tonight."

Sebastian grinned. "Fine by me."

She barked an order to her crew, and they picked up the pace and reboarded the Zodiac, although not without grumbling. As the winch was about to lower the boat to the ocean, an older man came out onto the deck.

Ellis stared. This was the first full drow she had seen among the soldiers on the Zodiac or the crew who had pulled them onto the deck. The drow ran up, gave Ellis a strange look, and pulled Sebastian aside. A moment later, the two men's voices disappeared. Ellis frowned. Their lips were moving, but not a single decibel of their conversation reached her. Neither had cast a muffling spell with shadow magic. Had someone else done it for them? She looked around but couldn't identify a nearby mage.

A blinking purple light drew Ellis' attention, and she saw that Sebastian was holding a device the size of a remote control. It had a glass bulb filled with swirling purple light on one end. Ellis' jaw dropped.

It was unmistakably shadow magic, yet she could see it. Bouncing on her toes with excitement, Ellis reached for the nearest deep shadows, which happened to be a shaded spot beneath the winch.

Nothing happened. Her shadow magic was as dead as ever. She looked back, and there it was again. Swirling purple magic.

Was it something about the glass? Was that what was casting the muffling spell?

A moment later, Sebastian confirmed her suspicions, holding up the device and flicking off a switch. The swirling purple glow disappeared, and his voice came back into her ears.

"Change in plans," he told Val, who had one leg in her wetsuit and was working on the second. Her expression turned homicidal. "I'm not jerking you around. Bring it in. We're going on red alert."

Her irritation vanished, replaced by grim professionalism.

"What's going on?" Ellis asked. Sebastian ignored her, but a red light began flashing on the deck, and a voice came over the speakers.

"We're going mobile in t-minus twenty, folks. Get your butts on the boards since it might be rocky for a few minutes."

Ellis' nausea deepened. As she reached into the bag for another ginger candy, she took comfort in the fact that her face was no longer at risk of turning bright red. *Bye-bye, tomato face. Hello...cucumber face? Romaine lettuce face? Cilantro face?* Thinking about food didn't help, so Ellis sprang into action. "You can't just sail away. You have to find Lola."

Sebastian sighed. "Five minutes ago, our radar picked up the USNS *Samantha* heading out to investigate the yacht fire. They'll be here in approximately twenty minutes."

"So? From what I've seen, there are a lot of powerful shadow mages on this ship. Can't you just make it invisible again? There's got to be someone here who can turn a little Zodiac invisible."

"There is, but that wouldn't solve the problem."

"What's the problem?"

"The *Samantha* is on a collision course with our present location. You ever hear about Newton's second law? Force equals mass times acceleration. I invite you to imagine what happens when eighteen thousand tons of boat decelerate on impact."

"Oh."

"'Oh' is right. You'd better get inside. And try lying on the floor while you're at it. It helps almost as much as the ginger."

CHAPTER TWO

Sebastian headed to the map room. Ellis declined to take his advice about lying down. Chewing ginger candy like her life depended on it, she staggered down the corridors until one of the crew took pity on her and escorted her to the medical bay. Inside, two physicians, three nurses, and Jerel were tending to the survivors from the torpedoed yacht.

"Motion sickness isn't at the top of our triage list," the nearest doctor said after taking a look at Ellis' face. The doctor was an efficient man in his early forties who clearly wasn't going to let his compassion for Ellis endanger his other patients. Although he appeared to be human, his glasses were drow. One of the lenses glowed with the purple light Ellis had seen on Sebastian's muffling device.

Ellis shook her head. "My mother. She's in here."

Across the room, Jerel looked up from adjusting the drip on an IV. "Ellis? Your mom's stable, but she won't wake for at least another day." He introduced Dr. Moray, the chief physician, who barely looked up from his work.

Ellis nodded, relieved. "How are the others doing?"

"I haven't lost anyone yet," Moray stated. "And I won't unless you keep bothering me."

Ellis nodded and returned to the hall, steeling herself for another move. Jerel ran after her.

"Here." He handed Ellis a small plastic bottle. She thought it was an airplane liquor bottle, but the fluid inside was a brownish-green, and it was hand-labeled in permanent marker as MS-112.

Ellis opened her mouth to ask about it, but the medic had left. Unscrewing the cap, she sniffed the contents. An earthy, fungal smell wafted out. She recognized familiar scents from her father's potions, although there were other ingredients she couldn't get a handle on.

Hoping that MS stood for "motion sickness," Ellis took a sip. Her nausea departed almost immediately. The rolling deck became an inconvenience rather than an assault, and she moved with a new confidence.

Sebastian hadn't assigned her any duties. He also hadn't restricted her movements. The sailors spared her little more than passing glances. So, she wasn't a prisoner. *I should look around before he changes his mind.*

The ship's layout was similar to the yacht's, so Ellis followed a hunch and made her way to the center. Finding double doors, she flung them open. "Bingo!"

She'd found the lounge, or rec room, or whatever you called it on a ship. It was small, with threadbare, comfortable sofas surrounding a ping-pong table. Shelves with mesh covers displayed stacks of board games and novels. In the corner, two people were playing Battleship.

"You're new," a small East Asian woman stated bluntly,

looking Ellis over. She had a sleek brown mohawk and introduced herself as Emily. "They fish you out of the yacht?"

Ellis nodded.

"You must be the captain's cousin. He's been looking for you." The other man was a drow with classic marine-blue skin and pale hair. "I'm Rami."

"Isn't the boat on red alert?" Ellis asked.

Rami snorted. "We're non-essential personnel." He and Emily exchanged bemused looks, and she added, "We should let them cook for themselves sometime. See how long they last before they change that designation."

"Emily's caramel custard is essential to life, in my opinion," Rami offered.

Hunger overtook Ellis, who was running on fumes, ginger candy, and whatever calories were in the motion sickness potion. "You haven't got any snacks in here, have you? Saltines, maybe?"

Rami looked horrified. "Saltines? *Saltines?* Would you ask Picasso for a finger painting?"

"I would," Ellis replied. "I could sell an original Picasso finger painting for a lot of money."

Rami groaned. "*Saltines.* Do you want dog food, too?"

"Maybe gruel," Emily added. "If Rami and I work hard enough, I'm sure we can blend a flavorless paste of some kind."

"Emily would never tell you this, but she used to have a Michelin star," Rami offered.

"You'd have one too if, well..."

"I'd have two if I was human." Rami grinned and focused on Ellis. "I've always wanted to share drow cuisine with the world. There is no umami quite like the umami of a mushroom-stuffed croissant."

Ellis' mouth watered. Operating on professional instinct, Emily tutted. "Look at us, jabbering about food while we let our guest starve. Come on, Rami. Let's introduce her to the belly of the *Violet Eel*."

They cheerfully clambered to their feet and dragged Ellis out of the break room toward what she assumed was the mess hall.

"Do you know what's in this?" Ellis asked, showing Rami the potion.

"Not in my sphere of knowledge. You'll have to ask Jerel. Seasick, mmm? No wonder your tank's empty. Well, now that you're feeling better, we'll fix that."

Ellis smiled weakly, hoping she was up to a Michelin-star meal. Jerel's wonder potion, as she had started to think of it over the last fifteen minutes, was holding fast.

The mess hall was a cozy, warm space near the engines, with an open kitchen at one end of a cafeteria. Rami pushed Ellis onto a bar stool, briefly conferred with Emily, and then announced they were making waffles.

"The leftovers can go into the bread pudding for dinner tomorrow, so we'll be more ahead than behind." Emily nodded.

As Ellis watched them work, good cheer took over her body. *This* was what she'd been trying to create at the Outpost, and this strange ship full of humans and drow had appeared out of thin air, having already mastered it.

"How..." Ellis started before falling silent. Questions competed for space in her brain, creating a pressure that made her skull feel like exploding.

"'How' is a start, but don't forget 'why' and 'where.'" Emily grinned as she handed a plastic tub of strawberries to Rami. "Would you mind?"

Rami accepted the tub and raised one hand. His fingers moved, weaving shadow magic, and the strawberries inside froze and shrank until they were the size of pennies.

"Want one?" Rami asked, offering Ellis the tub of now-freeze-dried berries. She took a slice. It was crunchy and pleasantly tart.

"Rami has really upped my freeze-drying game." Emily retrieved the strawberries and dumped them into a food processor. Soon, they were red powder. "Obviously, on a ship powered by shadow magic, refrigeration's not a problem."

Ellis' eyebrows went up. "Powered by shadow magic? Really?"

Emily pulled a carton of eggs out of an unusual refrigerator. Inside, thin, transparent tubes glowed with purple light. Not the kind of thing you could buy at Lowe's. "Not everything, and not exactly, but we do use a lot of it on the ship."

"If you can make the water behind a propellor blade disappear, you can make that blade turn," Rami explained. "If you wanna know more, you'll have to talk to the engineering team. I'm much more familiar with the kind of blade that peels potatoes."

"I saw a small device earlier," Ellis mused. "Sebastian was using it. It seemed like he was casting a muffling spell, but it was more mechanical than magical."

"We call them 'hush puppies,'" Emily explained.

"They're way more useful than muffling spells since anyone can use them," Rami added.

"We deploy them when someone complains about our food." Emily smirked.

Ellis gaped. "You mean, you've found a way for humans to use shadow magic?"

A memory of Charlie pushed its way into Ellis' consciousness, and her growing feeling of warm goodwill disappeared. She too had stumbled onto a way for a human to use shadow magic, and it had killed him. Ellis rubbed her eyes with her palms, willing her tears away.

"Whoa, you okay, there?" Emily asked. "Seasickness coming back?"

"No. I'm just tired."

"The captain's mum was a formidable spellcaster," Rami continued. "When Seb hit fourteen without showing a hint of the gift, she decided it was time for a more democratic approach to the use of shadow magic. It didn't help her with the ring problem, though."

Emily glared at Rami, whose mouth snapped shut.

"What ring problem?" Ellis asked.

"You'll have to talk to Seb about that." Rami was suddenly more subdued.

Ellis made several more attempts to garner information, but Rami had shut up tight. Emily was more cautious as well. Ten minutes later, the pair deposited a conversation-stopping pale pink waffle on the bar in front of Ellis, laden with whipped cream and lemon curd. Ellis, whose hunger had taken on monumental proportions, set the mystery aside and attacked the mountainous treat.

The food improved Ellis' physical condition, but her

good mood was gone. The truncated conversation reminded her that she knew next to nothing about this ship and its inhabitants. All she had to go on was Sebastian's claim that he was her cousin. That, and the evidence of drow-human collaboration she could see with her own eyes. She had to find a way off the ship so that she could deliver Claire's cure to her father.

As she tucked away the final bite, the red lights over both doors turned off. Rami and Emily exchanged looks, and Emily whisked away Ellis' plate before she could retrieve the final lingering dollop of lemon curd.

"It's been great to meet you, Ellis, but with the red alert downgraded, we're headed into the lunch rush. This is where folks on the *Eel* get their coffee, so everyone worth meeting will come by eventually. You can stick around if you want, but I need my counter space back."

Ellis knew a dismissal when she heard one. As a final kindness, Emily directed her toward the coffee, and soon Ellis was sitting at a table with a steaming mug as the crew of the *Violet Eel* streamed into the mess hall. Several gave her curious looks, but no one approached her. Finally, Ellis placed her mug on a bussing tray and left to find Sebastian.

Sebastian was in the map room, which was a large room on the top deck with windows looking out in three directions. When Ellis wandered in, Sebastian was hunched over a navigational chart, deep in conversation with one of his crew members. Finally, he looked up.

"Are you going back to the wreck?" she asked. "If Lola survived, we have to find her."

Sebastian shook his head. "No. We're staying out of it. The Navy's sending boats in to investigate, and it's too risky. I won't risk my people on the slim-to-none chance that she survived."

Ellis understood his perspective, but she couldn't let it go. "Give me a boat, and I'll do it. One of those rubber rafts, maybe."

"I'm willing to risk *your* life least of all," Sebastian countered. "And you told me you can't swim."

"You said that was normal."

"It is, but it doesn't make you a smart choice for amphibious missions. I'll happily provide you with swim lessons if I can drum up a three-day break between world-ending crises."

"You deal with a lot of those?" Ellis asked.

"That's our entire mandate. I imagine you can relate."

She could. "I won't be aboard long enough for swim lessons." Ellis sighed. "I have to get back to my dad."

Sebastian waved a hand. "I'll get that test tube to my science team, I promise."

Ellis wouldn't let it go. "Does that mean I am a prisoner?"

"You're not in a cell, are you?"

"A ship-sized prison is still a prison," Ellis snapped.

When Sebastian was frustrated, his freckles turned a deeper shade of violet. "If you want to think of yourself as a prisoner, be my…well, not my *guest,* I suppose. My *detainee.* The nomenclature doesn't matter to me. I saved your butt from a burning ocean, so you can be grateful or not."

"Well, I'm not. *You* torpedoed the yacht!"

The freckles were now mauve and getting darker. "Like I said, I didn't give that order lightly. From the chatter, it sounded like the team on the yacht might be nearing the production of a viable transmissible bacteria strain. Would you sacrifice yourself if it meant saving the world?"

"Of course," Ellis answered immediately.

"That was what I assumed, but I'm sorry I had to make that choice for you. We're not perfect, but we do our best. Marusya Klimova got *very* close to releasing a bio bomb at the peace summit, so everyone's been on edge. That was a massive intelligence and operational failure, and I didn't need you saving my ass a second time."

Ellis smiled at the compliment, but she wondered how realistic Sebastian's goals were. "You can't stop *every* bad thing ever from happening."

"Not with that attitude," Sebastian replied, and a small smile crept across his face. "You're right, but the *Violet Eel* tries to stop the genuine catastrophes."

"So, you're vigilantes? You're the…the Ellis Burton of the seas?"

His grin widened. "A little egotistical, no?"

"Hey, like you said. I stopped Marusya when you couldn't."

"I suppose that's fair."

Sebastian made her feel like she'd known him for years. She had just met him, but the set of his shoulders and the line of his mouth were familiar.

She put a finger on it. "Nan Elandra." Sebastian

reminded her of her grandmother. "She's your grandmother, too."

He deflated like it was an accusation. "That's right, but I don't have any photos. Mum tried to draw her for me once, but she was a terrible artist." He chuckled at the memory.

"Your mom. Is she..."

"She's dead," Sebastian stated. "Did you know she was responsible for ending the Cold War?"

"What! How?"

"I can't cough up all the *Eel*'s secrets on your first day. Stick around, and someday, I'll tell you the whole story. I don't mean to seem callous about your father. I really don't. Mum died of pneumonia if you can believe it. Picked it up on her last mission. Lowered resistance because of growing up in a cave. That's one of our biggest hurdles. I take infectious diseases *very* seriously, which is why I can't take any chances with that test tube."

Ellis thought about Nan and the circumstances that had led to her and Sebastian being here. Her eyes welled.

"Are you all right?" Sebastian asked.

"Yes. I just miss her. Nan Elandra, that is. I wish I could talk to her about all this." Ellis sighed.

"She'd be interested to see it. At least, I hope she would."

"How...how did this happen? The ship, I mean. All these people."

Sebastian waved her to a chair and sat down.

"As you can imagine from knowing her, your grandmother had a wild youth," Sebastian began.

Ellis smiled. That was true. Even as a very old woman, she'd been wild. She'd also accepted Ellis without reservations.

"When she was about your age, which was a good hundred years ago, she left the Homestead and went to Los Angeles with her friend Chari. She is still alive, by the way, but very old and not very well. She lives at an estate we maintain on one of the San Juan islands. Anyway, that's beside the point. Elandra and Chari arrived in Los Angeles, and they associated with the fringes of human society. They lived with a group of humans for two years. Long enough for Elandra to have my mum."

"Your grandfather was a human?" Ellis asked.

Sebastian nodded. No wonder Nan had accepted Ellis. *Why didn't she tell me?*

"But how…how did they live? Why aren't there reports in any of the newspapers? Did my dad know he had a sister?"

"I don't think so. One of the conditions of leaving was that she never tell anyone about what happened. Although I suppose it's possible. People age. Defenses slip. Can your dad keep a secret?"

"Oh, yes." Ellis her mood darkened. For much of her life, keeping secrets was *all* her father had done.

"Well, then, who knows? We can ask him how the *humans* kept it quiet. Elandra and Chari were living with a group of magicians. Not shadow mages. I mean occultists: Alastair Crowley, Jack Parsons, and their crew. Also a bunch of spooky dudes from the Jet Propulsion Lab who were into summoning demons and what have you. A lot of this is widely known, but people think the magic bit was fake."

"It wasn't."

"Not all of it. Elandra and Chari worked with the JPL

scientists on understanding what shadow magic was all about. Long story short, no one knows what it is. The smartest people in the world couldn't crack that one. Nonetheless, they were able to create many useful magical applications. The seeds of what would eventually grow into the *Violet Eel*."

"They weren't being experimented on, were they? I mean, against their will?" Ellis asked. "Chari and Elandra?"

"No. Elandra left diaries. They're...spicy. She was in love."

That was a relief. Well, not the spicy diary bit. There were things about your grandmother you simply didn't need to know.

"How much do you know about my dad?" she asked. "About what happened between him and my mother? What do you know about the DRI?"

"We knew they existed, but they were a tiny research institute without much visible output. We didn't know they were holding drow captive."

Ellis searched his face for the tells of a lie. She thought he was telling the truth, but she needed more assurance. "No one's being held here or experimented on against their will, are they?" she asked.

"We don't press people into service, no. The *Violet Eel* has a free crew. People come and go, although once they meet me, they tend to stay. It's my charisma and leadership." He flashed a wide smile.

"Don't forget about your humility," Ellis muttered.

"I don't believe in false humility. Although, if you want to get in the weeds, I guess I'm not the big draw. I've hired the best people in the world in every area. That's why people join the *Eel*."

"Like Emily with her Michelin star?" Ellis asked.

"She never brings that up. You must have met Rami."

"They made me a waffle."

"And?"

Ellis nodded. "You've recruited good people. Exceptionally good people. But I still don't really understand what you do."

"Aside from cooking the best waffles in the world?"

"Yes."

"Our three main efforts are research, intelligence, and ops. I'm not going to tell you much about our research arm, but you're not stupid, so you can probably guess."

"The magic refrigerators. And the goggles. And the cloaking spell on the ship, or whatever turned it invisible. And the hush puppies."

Sebastian raised an eyebrow. "Tsk tsk! Loose lips. But I suppose there's no harm in knowing the *name* of a thing you've already seen."

"You're combining shadow magic and human technology," Ellis ventured.

Sebastian looked at her carefully. "Like I said, that's a conversation for another time. Next, there's intelligence. A certain amount of classic espionage. I'm sure you can imagine a range of scenarios where shadow magic is useful for information gathering. The *Eel* has agents in major cities. DC, Beijing, Moscow, and Cairo, among others. We also do extensive digital surveillance."

"What, exactly, are you looking for?" Ellis asked.

"World-ending events. For example, Marusya's virus.

We also keep an eye out for drow exposure events. Like, for instance, the kind of very unusual surveillance footage that might show up after a bank robbery." His eyes sparkled, although his voice was mild.

"We weren't stealing *money,*" Ellis stated peevishly.

"Why not? We do," Sebastian countered.

Ellis' jaw dropped. "What?"

"Come *on*. If the stories about your grandmother are true, she was the sworn enemy of a locked door."

"I guess that's true." Ellis wished she still had Nan's moonsteel picks.

"There's an old saying. A boat is a hole in the ocean you pour money into. Well, you know what a ship is?" Ellis waited patiently. Sebastian was clearly enjoying himself. "It's a really, really, *really* big hole."

"A hole you fill with what, gold bars?"

"That's your trademark, not ours."

Ellis suddenly felt uneasy. She didn't like the idea that someone had been tracking her every move. "You've been spying on me."

"A bit," Sebastian acknowledged. "Not all the time. God knows we missed the Klimova debacle. But we knew a drow vigilante was operating in Los Angeles. It took us a long time to track you down because we didn't expect..."

"What?"

"We didn't expect you to look human. We'd kept tabs on most mixed-heritage people. Rami calls us *pastels,* but I'm not sure I'm on board with that. Anyway, we were surprised. I suppose we shouldn't have assumed we were the only group of part-drow."

"I'm hardly a *group*," Ellis stated. Much of her life had been lonely.

"You might be the only mixed person around, but you've assembled plenty of acolytes. The Outpost is..."

"Impressive?"

"I was going to say, 'a problem.'"

Ellis bristled at the dismissive tone. "Such a big problem that we took out Marusya Klimova when you couldn't."

"And then you lost her," Sebastian pointed out mildly.

"We took down the DRI!" Ellis exclaimed.

He sighed. "I'll give you that one. Here on the *Violet Eel*, we've built a Ferrari. You're out in the boonies, trying to invent the wheel."

Ellis' face turned bright red, and she wished that she was still seasick. "What do *you* do that's so great?"

"I was about to tell you about our third arm, ops. I suspect that is your strong suit."

"I do like kicking stuff," Ellis admitted.

Sebastian grinned. "Surveillance identifies targets, and we take action."

"What kind of action?"

"Anything that serves our mission."

"Which is?"

"Our primary mission is to protect humankind, the drow, and particularly the areas where humans and drow encounter one another."

"Does that mean you have a *secondary* mission?"

"You're sharp. I like that. It's high time we brought you into the fold."

"Maybe I don't want to be folded in. Maybe I want to do my own thing."

Sebastian's expression darkened, and he didn't respond. "Unless you plan to swim home, you might as well try to enjoy yourself. Talk to the crew. Make up your own mind."

"About *what?*" Ellis demanded. There was something he wasn't telling her, and apparently, he wasn't going to.

Sebastian texted someone, and a moment later, a young drow woman appeared at the door. "Ready to see your quarters?" she asked.

"You should sleep," Sebastian said.

Ellis shrugged. "Yeah. Maybe."

The young drow woman introduced herself as Peri and led Ellis into the bowels of the ship. When she faced a familiar door, her unease had little to do with seasickness.

"You okay?" Peri asked.

Ellis nodded, but internally, prepared to run. The space was nearly identical to her cell on the yacht. Her hesitation eased when Peri knocked and flung open the door with a cheerful "Halooooo."

As on the yacht, the room contained four bunks. Unlike on the yacht, these bunks were strewn with clothes, books, and electronics. The walls had been painted with cheerful orange and yellow stripes, and pictures and photos covered every available surface.

There was only one person in the room. Ellis thought from the faint sharpness of her ears that she might be part drow, but it was difficult to be sure. She wore large dark glasses, and she looked up with curiosity as Peri introduced Ellis.

"That's Mara," Peri greeted.

"Did you bring any books?" Mara asked eagerly, scooting to the edge of her bunk.

"Don't be stupid, Mara. They fished her out of the burning wreckage. Why would she have a book?"

"She could have a wet book," Mara muttered.

"No books," Ellis replied. "Sorry."

"We've got pretty much everything in the library, but I can't stand reading on my tablet. Light sensitivity. Not great for someone born in Los Angeles, but it's better now that I work mostly belowdecks."

"Mara's on the science team. Keiko went home for a few weeks, so we're putting you in her bunk," Peri announced, pointing at the top right-hand corner. Ellis wasn't sure how she was going to sleep with Peri and Mara chattering at each other.

A moment later, Peri handed her a hush puppy and a black silk sleep mask. "You look like you're ready for a good eight hours."

"Maybe twelve," Ellis admitted.

"It's not exactly privacy." Peri rattled the device. "But it's useful. We can find the bosun and get you kitted out with pajamas and whatnot, but you look like you'd rather fall asleep in what you're wearing."

Ellis looked down. Her clothes had dried, but her heavy boots were still wet. She tried to remember the last time she'd taken them off.

"Maybe not my boots," she said and set about unlacing them. Then she crawled into the bunk. She spent several minutes clicking the switch on the hush puppy on and off, listening as Peri's and Mara's voices popped in and out.

She would have taken the device apart if she'd found a way to open it, but none of the seams yielded to her prying fingernails. Finally, exhaustion extinguished her curiosity, and Ellis fell asleep, rocked by the waves.

CHAPTER THREE

Charlie didn't want to die in a car crash. He was worried about that because Percy was staring through the moon roof again, trying to catch sight of the big albatross that was acting as the car's scout. Unfortunately, Percy was also driving.

"Watch it!" Charlie exclaimed as the wheels veered onto the rumble strips. Percy glanced down only long enough to bring the car back between the lines.

"Pull over," Charlie ordered. "You birdwatch, I'll drive."

Percy poked the rearview mirror. It set the orange plastic rhino dangling from the device to swaying. "Cain't."

"It'll only take a second."

Percy winced, and the car accelerated. "We don't have a second. According to Mariner..." that was the albatross, "we've got unmarked black cars on our tail, and if I stop pushing the pedal, they'll catch up right quick."

There was a low scoff from the back, and Mikhail Klimova leaned between the seats. "If this is high-speed chase situation, I should drive." He sounded enthusiastic about the possibility. Rose, in the seat next to him, rolled her eyes. When she'd learned they were going to rescue Percy, she'd gotten in her car and raced out to the desert. When they'd found him, she was the first one he'd greeted. Their connection was strong.

Dust on the rear window blocked the view of the only vehicle behind them, a fourteen-wheeler. Charlie glanced at the kid, but he trusted Percy. Or rather, he trusted Percy's animal spy network, as unconventional as it was.

Finding Percy in the desert had been surprisingly easy. When they'd stopped for gas in Twenty-nine Palms, a large black crow had landed on the windshield. It had momentarily hopped out of the way when Charlie had swiped at it with a squeegee but otherwise stayed put.

When the crow dug its claws into the wiper as Charlie accelerated out of the lot, he'd sensed that something was up.

"You want us to follow you?" Charlie had asked, stopping the car. The crow had squawked. Interpreting the animal's directions had not been entirely straightforward, but eventually, Charlie had gotten his car pointed at a cluster of rural houses on the north side of Yucca Valley. Warned that they were coming, Percy had met them on the road. It was only when he explained what had happened that the sirens in the distance started to look like a problem.

"We can't outrace the cops," Charlie stated. "They have more resources than we do."

"Who is it?" Rose asked. "If it's cops, I might have enough leverage to talk us out of a speeding ticket."

Percy's face was briefly uneasy, then went studiously

neutral again. Rose had run a high quality brothel out of Santa Monica for several decades, and Charlie assumed plenty of important people had spilled their guts to her.

Percy cleared his throat. "It's not cops, and it's not something a, uh…pretty face can get us out of. As pretty as that face is," he added, beaming. Rose smiled shyly. That seemed to annoy Mikhail, who believed he should be the sole focus of any beautiful and/or maternal woman in a ten-mile radius. Rose was both.

There was a flash of black as a small cluster of birds appeared on the horizon. Mariner circled them, agitated.

"Shit!" Percy exclaimed, and the tires hit the rumble strip again.

Mikhail turned around as several black dots appeared on the road in the distance.

Percy cautioned. "No, girl! Don't you dare. You can't fight a whirlybird, and you won't, not on my behalf."

A bird squawked overhead. Mariner didn't like being told what to do any more than Percy.

"Helicopters?" Charlie asked. Percy nodded and kept nodding, squirming in his seat.

"There is plan?" Mikhail asked, sounding hopeful.

The answer was silence. The cars behind them were getting closer.

Should he try to make them invisible? Charlie wasn't sure he could. Not the whole car, and not for very long. Not in the middle of the day. Maybe if they pulled off… They should have done that minutes ago before they were in full view of their tail.

Whoever their attackers were, he didn't want to alert them to his shadow magic abilities. He was Charlie

Morrissey, a former police detective. That should carry some weight to the other badges. He hoped.

"We should just talk to them," Charlie stated. "We're just four friends on a drive. We're not doing anything illegal, right? I mean, if you're carrying a brick of heroin, now's the time to speak up."

"I have bubblegum vape," Mikhail offered more cheerfully than Charlie appreciated.

Rose grimaced. "That *should* be illegal." The jab appeared to genuinely wound her seatmate.

"If they arrest us for *anything,* lawyer up," Charlie warned. It hurt his cop's soul to give them this warning, but Percy, Mikhail, and Rose had all been engaged in criminal activity of one kind or another. They were in a country with laws and civil rights. They would be okay.

Percy pulled the car onto the shoulder. He kept it running to leave the A/C on, and there was a tense minute while a black van and two unmarked BMWs caught up with them from behind. A helicopter flew in from up ahead.

Charlie knew cops. He could deal with cops. The men who got out of the van were not cops, or not normal ones. They were fully armored and carried automatic weapons.

That's not good. As they approached the car, Charlie realized he'd made a terrible mistake.

Shots rang out, and for a moment, he was sure they'd been hit. There was a low hiss, and the car sank beneath them. The soldiers had shot the tires out.

"Move *very* slowly," Charlie whispered. "Don't reach for anything. No sudden movements."

Then the soldiers were on top of them. The silence in

the car exploded into chaos as the first soldier opened the door with a yell. Hands grabbed Charlie, and everything went sideways. His face was pressed into burning asphalt in the hundred-degree sun. Mariner cried overhead, and Percy shouted, "Don't you dare!" at the top of his lungs.

Charlie couldn't tell if Percy was talking to the soldiers or the birds, and he never found out because a black bag was slung over his head. At first, it was a relief from the burning ground, but then he was yanked to his feet by many pairs of hands. Plastic bit into his wrists as someone applied zip-ties to secure his hands behind him.

A burst of cold air hit the exposed triangle of skin at his neck, which told him he was near another vehicle. The men at his elbows threw him onto a hard metal surface. In the following moments, three more bodies landed near or on top of him, and the door slammed.

"You didn't read us our Miranda rights!" Charlie shouted. There was no response. No one had even heard him. After a moment, the black van vibrated across the rumble strips, pulling back onto the road.

"Is everyone okay?" Charlie asked. Rose and Percy made small affirmative noises, and Mikhail shouted Russian curses.

At least they were alive, he told himself. A few hours later, he wasn't as happy about that. If hell existed, he thought it might feel like this. He could have tolerated either the pain or the boredom, but the combination was terrible. There was nothing to focus on except the plastic biting into his wrists. His face hurt too, the asphalt burns blistering. The soldiers had pressed his cheek into the surface *hard*.

If Charlie had trusted himself enough to use shadow magic blind in a confined space, he would have. However, he was afraid he'd dissolve his hands along with the plastic handcuffs.

After what seemed like an eternity, Rose said, "Ugh, for Pete's sake." There was movement at Charlie's feet as bodies wiggled. What was happening? Surely not an escape attempt. Three seconds later, Rose told him to hold still. Her face got very close to his, and then the light pressure on his neck was released and the bag slid up and over his head.

Rose spit out the black fabric and grinned at him. "I've removed more complicated clothing than this with my teeth," she stated proudly.

Charlie laughed, and Percy indulgently smiled at her as she got to work on Mikhail.

Unfortunately, being able to see did nothing to improve their situation. The back of the van was tightly sealed, a box with an overhead light and a few A/C vents. Percy's face was as badly burned as Charlie's. Mikhail, who had put up the most resistance, had a split lip and a black eye that worsened by the mile. Fortunately, Rose had been treated more gently.

"I don't think we're being arrested," Percy offered.

Charlie nodded at the glittering black eye of a security camera next to the overhead light. "I spy with my little eye."

Percy got it. *Someone's watching. Don't talk about anything important.* Every so often, Percy's face became remote, as if he were listening to a song on invisible earphones. Charlie guessed he was linking with his animal network. They might have some idea of where they were going. He wished Percy could share that information but couldn't risk asking.

"Let's go on road trip," Mikhail muttered. "Will be fun."

CHAPTER FOUR

A violent wave of nausea woke Ellis, and she scrambled in her pocket for the ginger candies and the bottle of seasickness potion. Healthy doses of both calmed her, and she climbed out of bed. The digital clock on the wall told her it was ten a.m., and she was alone in the room. A glance through the porthole told her the ship was still underway.

Ellis panicked. What if Sebastian was taking them away from Los Angeles? For all she knew, they were headed to Australia or the North Pole, putting more distance between her father and the cure he badly needed. She resolved to petition the captain for help again.

Ellis headed to the medical bay first. Jerel was tending to Claire and one of the Russian guards, both of whom were shackled to their hospital beds by one foot.

"Why is my mother restrained?" Ellis demanded.

"Because she's going to regain consciousness soon," Jerel explained. "And I have orders to treat her as a hostile noncombatant."

"She's only hostile to people who stand in the way of her ambitions or who she thinks are stupid." Ellis sighed. "Which is a lot of people."

"Seb said you'd come to check on her before anything else. Very perceptive, our captain."

"Where's Mirelle?" Ellis asked.

"Medically cleared and moved to the brig. She's in one of the shadow-proof cells. Seb told me to give you your assignment for today."

"My *assignment?*"

"We're a working vessel, not a luxury cruise. No shuffleboard on the Lido Deck."

"The captain told me he didn't press-gang new sailors."

Jerel snorted. "I'm supposed to tell you the assignment is voluntary, but between you and me, don't shirk if you're not sick. Not if you want to make friends."

Ellis glanced at the shackle on her mother's ankle. *Who says I want to make friends?*

"Are you going to give me more of your magic seasickness potion, or is my vomit one of the things I have to swab off the decks?"

Without comment, Jerel fished around in a cabinet and produced a small vial, which he tossed to her. "You're not swabbing the decks."

"No? Am I doing something worse? Bilge duty? Bad news. I don't even know what a bilge is."

"You're not on bilge duty. Go find Rami and Em. They'll set you up."

"Can I say hi first?" Ellis asked, nodding at her mother.

"Of course. Although she probably can't hear you."

Ellis went over to her mother. She was hooked to several IVs, so Ellis put her hand on Claire's leg, squeezing it lightly.

"I'm going to get your cure to Dad. I promise." Ellis sat for a moment in companionable silence. Jerel and the doctors returned to work, and Ellis saw that a drawer was open. Inside, a pair of steel restraints—the kind the med team was using on Mirelle and the Russian guard—gleamed.

When she decided no one was watching, she removed the cuffs, slipping them into the band of her pants in two places so they wouldn't clank. Then, she pulled her sweatshirt down over them.

Rami was ripping pink waffles into chunks in large metal catering trays when Ellis came in. He smiled.

"I guess I've got KP duty," Ellis said.

"Not exactly," Rami replied. He directed her to a tray of breakfast sandwiches under a heat lamp at the side of the room.

"What do you want me to do with these?" Ellis asked.

"I want you to eat one. You look like you need fuel."

The sandwich was predictably excellent. When she was done, Rami solicited her help in dousing the shredded waffles with custard. When the soon-to-be-bread-pudding was in the refrigerator, he led her to a door at the back of the kitchen, then down several flights of stairs and into a large, cool chamber.

The second the door cracked open, Ellis smelled where she was. The low, rich notes of the decomposing growth medium filled her nose, and she smiled at the sight of row upon row of mushrooms in all stages of growth. "This is nice!"

"Yeah. Captain Seb's intel says you are a pro mycologist."

"Pro? I don't know if I'd go that far." Ellis was distracted by an electronic readout showing temperature and humidity readings. They weren't giving some of their trumpet varietals enough moisture.

"What do you say? Willing to help out down here for the next few weeks?"

"I won't be on the ship that long," Ellis murmured, adjusting a dial.

Rami looked uncomfortable. "I've been having trouble with a new strain of rustcaps. Could you take a look?"

Ellis schooled her face into a pleasant smile as her heart beat faster in her chest. The dim glow of the overhead lights felt harsh and the shadows cast by the mushrooms felt more menacing. *Was* she a prisoner?

Sebastian seemed well-intentioned, but they had very different priorities. Ellis struggled to concentrate on Rami's words as he chattered about the grow room's nanoclimate regions and genetic mycological work. Ellis had never seen a few of the species since some were from different parts of the world. Others, she suspected, were genetically engineered strains unique to the *Violet Eel*. Her eyes landed on a crop of tall purple mushrooms with very thin stems that grew in riotous S-curves.

"I call those 'Violet Eels.' I was trying to make the ship a namesake mushroom." Rami picked one and handed it to Ellis.

"What do they do?"

"Make the best stroganoff you've ever tasted."

Ellis attempted a smile, but she felt cold and alone. She needed time to think. She bit into the mushroom, comforted by the squeak and the earthy, savory flavors. "I'm happy to help out." She would decide if it was a lie later.

Rami beamed. He spent the next half-hour walking her through the mushroom cultivation process. The grow room ran itself, and any real improvements would take weeks, if not months, to implement. Rami seemed to think she'd have the time, which wasn't a good sign.

What did Sebastian want from her? Her silence, for one. Plenty of world governments would be happy to learn about the existence of a magical transnational vigilante force. Senator Chan, for example. Ellis wondered what the senator would say about the *Eel*.

Maybe Sebastian was making sure he could trust her. He hadn't put her in the brig, but maybe that was because he never intended her to leave. He cared about the world in a remote, utilitarian way. That was a luxury she didn't have.

When Rami went back to the kitchen, Ellis got to work. First, she made a mental catalog of the mushroom species on the boat. The grow operation didn't have everything, but it had a lot. She might not be able to swim, but she could arm herself for an attempt to leave the boat.

Ellis retrieved a spray bottle from the side of the room, dumped it out, rinsed it well, and refilled it a quarter of the way with rubbing alcohol. Then she began adding mushrooms. She wished she had the recipe for Lola's knockout powder, but that would require a workshop and a week of dehydrating. Rami could have done it in a few minutes, but asking him for help would raise questions.

When Ellis thought she had achieved the right mix, she sat on the floor, swirling the spray bottle. The rubbing alcohol would extract the active compounds from the mushrooms. After half an hour, Ellis put the spray bottle down and set about doing something that might reasonably look like work. She harvested the largest mushrooms from the trays, neatly depositing her haul into collection bins. These bins had thin metal handles, and during a break, Ellis pried two off. The metal bent without breaking, and she dropped them into her pocket.

Slipping the spray bottle under her sweatshirt, Ellis carried the trays up to the kitchen. Rami and Emily were elbow-deep in a complicated-looking lasagna recipe and didn't seem eager to interrogate her about her activities.

After depositing the trays, Ellis found her way back to her bunk. Peri was asleep, a glowing hush puppy dangling from a hook above her bunk. Double-checking to make sure the woman's eyes were closed, Ellis mussed her covers and slipped the spray bottle and handcuffs and handles underneath. From the state of this room, she doubted the ship had a housekeeping crew.

Then she went up top. Now that she had a handle on her seasickness, she was better able to appreciate the ocean. To someone who had grown up in a cave, it seemed impossibly vast. An endless stretch of water, sky, and light. Did the drow crew ever find it difficult to bear? Probably not the ones who stayed.

The ship had dropped anchor, and a small knot of sailors were headed toward the Zodiac winch with fishing equipment. Trying to look inconspicuous, Ellis wandered over and watched them release the raft from its cradle. The longer she watched, the more hopeless she felt. The winch needed two people to operate.

I can figure that out later. Maybe Mirelle would help in exchange for a ride back to shore. The thought of springing one of Marusya Klimova's collaborators made Ellis queasy, and she put it aside. She watched as one of the sailors shifted the motor into neutral, pushed a lever at the side of the wheel down, squeezed the clutch, and adjusted the gearshift. The Zodiac lurched forward on the waves. Not so different from a motorcycle, so she could manage it in a crisis. *When am I* not *in a crisis?*

Knowing how to steer a boat wouldn't help if she didn't know where to go. *I could navigate by the sun and stars like a seventeenth-century sea captain.* Ellis looked up. The sun was almost directly overhead. If she started in the early morning, she'd be able to figure out which direction was east. She had to hope that the *Eel* had stayed close to shore. Based on what Sebastian had told her about their mission, she doubted it would head into the middle of the ocean for no reason.

Ellis joined the crew for lunch and dinner. When she thought no one was looking, she slipped two extra apples into her pocket. It wasn't much in the way of provisions, but it was better than nothing. The real concern would be water, and she could not ask around for a large jug without attracting attention. She would have to figure that out tonight. Ellis' plan felt more preposterous by the minute, but she had to press forward.

After dinner, Ellis napped for several hours, claiming a recurring bout of seasickness. As the rest of the crew, or the ones who weren't on night duty, settled in, she forced her eyes to stay open and waited. When her cabin mates were dead asleep, Ellis grabbed her hush puppy, flicked it on, and threw it into her pillowcase with the spray bottle of mushroom juice and the pilfered handcuffs. She was as well-prepared as a runaway teen, but she would make it work.

She wished the *Violet Eel* had developed a way to turn a person invisible without shadow magic. Something like the hush puppy. Maybe they had built such a device, and they were keeping it a secret. She would have to get into the science department using old-fashioned stealth.

Few doors on the *Violet Eel* were locked. The science department was the exception. Ellis retrieved the flexible metal handles she'd stolen from the grow room and got to work on the locks. They weren't complicated, and after a few minutes, she heard the telltale click. Moving carefully, Ellis pushed the door open.

The small lab just inside the doors was impeccable. It was also occupied. A drow woman was using an eyedropper to meticulously transfer the liquid in an amber glass bottle into a glowing purple solution. She was focused on her work, and the hush puppy muffled the opening door. Ellis guiltily wrapped her fingers around her spray bottle and crept forward.

When she was three paces away, the researcher held up

the amber glass bottle and froze as the glass reflected Ellis' motion.

"Shit!" Ellis raised her bottle and sprayed, realizing too late that her opponent was wearing safety goggles. She sprayed again, aiming for the woman's mouth. The scientist spat, carefully aiming away from her experiment, but it was too late. She had inhaled the fungal spray. Ellis cheered inwardly as the woman's pupils increased to the size of saucers.

The liquid wasn't poisonous in the conventional sense. Ellis had created a combination she'd gauged as both safe and potent. Rustcaps increased the speed at which the mixture entered an opponent's bloodstream. Sleeper morels, a potent sedative, slowed movement. Finally, she'd added enough hallucinogens to make an elephant see a god.

"It's *you,*" the woman stated.

Oh, shit. Does she think I'm a god? The researcher was staring at her with wide-eyed adoration.

"You're the ringbearer! The Great Uniter!"

"I assure you that I am not." Ellis didn't have time to think about the ominous pronouncement because the open amber glass dropper bottle was shaking in the woman's gloved hand. *Next time, drug people* after *they put down the open bottles of dangerous chemicals.*

"I command you to put down that bottle!" Ellis attempted to sound like the Mother Beneath, not that she knew what the subterranean deity's voice sounded like. While Ellis had occasionally prayed, she'd never gotten a reply. Uncertain if she should pitch her voice higher or lower, she wound up doing both. If she was a god, she was a god going through puberty. The researcher frowned, and with a disquieting slowness, started to drop the bottle into the beaker of glowing purple liquid.

Ellis' addition of the sleeper morels paid off, and she was able to snatch the bottle just before it fell. Placing it gently on the table and re-capping it, she led the researcher over to the wall and handcuffed her to a fume hood bolted to the floor.

"Am I dead?" the woman asked. Her pupils had eclipsed her irises, which were now a slim blue corona around the black pits of her pupils. After a moment, she screamed at the top of her lungs, sending Ellis stumbling back against a nearby cabinet. Fortunately, she was still in the envelope created by Ellis' hush puppy.

She would have to leave the hush puppy here. There was no way around it.

Ellis put the device on top of the fume hood, which she judged to be just out of the stoned scientist's reach. Then, she squeezed the woman's shoulder.

"Sorry to send you on a surprise vacation from reality." Ellis tried to sound soothing. "Um. You're safe. You're loved. And hopefully, you're about to gain some meaningful lifelong insights into your psyche. Good luck!"

Ellis patted the shoulder and stood, intent on finding the test tube containing her father's cure. The first five minutes of her search were futile, and she was starting to wonder if she would need to enlist the scientist's help. The test tube had been double-sealed in clear plastic and placed at the back of a fridge, behind a sub sandwich Ellis commandeered for her bindle. Her search also turned up a two-gallon jug of water.

Thank you, science. She threw the jug and the test tube into the pillowcase, slung it on her shoulder, gripped her spray bottle of psychedelic mushroom juice, and headed for the boats.

There were no security patrols on the deck, and by some miracle, Ellis reached the Zodiac without incident. She took a deep breath, realizing she hadn't expected to get this far.

Shit. What was she going to do about the boat? Ellis unclipped the protective cover to reveal the raft. She could not operate the winch on her own, but she had to get the Zodiac in the water. Releasing it from its cradle, she tested its weight. Only a few hundred pounds. If she had a long enough rope, she could lower it into the ocean.

She didn't have a rope. She had nothing but herself and a half-assed plan.

Half an ass is better than no asses.

With a sick grin, Ellis braced herself and kicked the Zodiac out of its cradle. It teetered on the edge of the deck for a moment, then freewheeled toward the water below.

By some miracle, it landed right-side up, bumped the ship twice, and then drifted away on a current.

The water was fifty feet below her. She would survive the drop if she had a life vest. Fortunately, the ship was well-equipped—a possible side effect of having many weak swimmers onboard.

Opening a nearby cabinet, Ellis selected a likely-looking vest. Buckling the orange foam around her torso, she gripped the pillowcase tight. After a moment, she reconsidered, pulled the spray bottle out, and set it on the deck. The med team would probably appreciate knowing what their crewmate had been dosed with.

She was stalling. *No. I'm not stalling. I'm just waiting for the right moment to fling myself and my pillowcase four stories into the freezing and probably shark-infested ocean.* Shivering, she stepped toward the rail.

As the metal shook under her boot, something warm and soft fell on her shoulder. Ellis screamed and dove for the spray bottle, but it was too late. Black-clad figures popped into existence beside her, and strong hands pulled her away from the rail.

"*Stop! Help!*" she screeched, an image of her father's pale, shriveling face flashing through her mind as she struggled against her abductors. If she could just fling herself over the rail…

"Ellis! It's over!" Sebastian's clear, firm voice cut through the chaos, and Ellis sagged. The soldiers at her sides pulled her straight, and she stared into Sebastian's craggy, disappointed face. His freckles blazed an angry purple as he glanced over the rail in annoyance.

"If you don't know how to fix a Zodiac, you'll learn," he growled, snapping his fingers. Several soldiers rushed forward.

"Suit up and go fish it out." Sebastian pointed at the bobbing boat. After raking Ellis with reproachful looks, they went to retrieve wetsuits from a nearby storage compartment.

"How did you catch me?" Ellis asked. It was a stupid question. Her plan had been slapdash, a desperate Hail Mary that even she had been surprised to see go as far as it had.

"If you rescued someone with uncertain loyalties whom you nonetheless hoped to befriend, what would *you* do?"

"Set a powerful shadow mage on them," Ellis muttered grudgingly.

"Right. You're not stupid, and neither am I. I am, however, very disappointed. If you poisoned Corinne, there will be severe consequences. What was in that bottle you sprayed her with?"

Defensively, Ellis described the mixture of sedatives and hallucinogens. "She'll be fine. Well, I'm pretty sure she will."

"She'd better be," Sebastian growled. "So, after you, a woman who admittedly *cannot swim,* flung yourself into the Pacific Ocean, what was your plan?"

"Climb into the Zodiac, get to shore, and save my father."

"Where does the two-gallon bottle of rubbing alcohol come in?" Sebastian asked.

"What?"

He held up the two-gallon jug from her pillowcase. Ellis blanched.

"You thought it was water," Sebastian mused.

"I-I thought..."

"That you should thank me for saving you from dying of wood alcohol poisoning in the middle of the Pacific? Yes, you should."

Ellis kept her mouth shut.

"Rami said you were going to keep me prisoner for weeks, maybe months. My dad does not have that long."

"He said that?"

"No, but I can tell."

"Dying of exposure in the middle of the Atlantic wouldn't help your father."

Ellis waited, sure someone was about to slap cuffs on her and haul her to the brig. Instead, Sebastian stood at the rail with his hands on his hips.

"Drop anchor," he barked at a nearby sailor. "It's time we had a senior officers' meeting."

CHAPTER FIVE

As the mess hall filled, Ellis got a true sense of the *Eel*'s eclecticism. The three tables nearest to the kitchen were packed with drow and humans from all over the world. The captain hadn't restrained her after her escape attempt, but the two large drow men sitting on either side of her at one of the front tables twitched whenever she moved. Rami, who apparently counted as senior staff, produced vats of coffee, which marginally improved the simmering atmosphere of half-awake annoyance.

"Is this a trial?" Ellis asked.

"No," Sebastian snapped, then ignored her further questions. When Rami put a mug of coffee in front of her, she sipped it peevishly.

When a physician hustled in from the medical unit, Sebastian nodded and climbed to his feet.

"You all know Ellis," Sebastian began. "Our LA vigilante. Head of the Outpost project. Most recently took out the DRI, and foiled Marusya Klimova's first global bioweapon plot."

Ellis swelled with pride at this description of her skills, sitting up straighter.

"Ellis is requesting to return to shore to deliver a treatment developed by Claire Burton to three drow currently in medical quarantine in the Outpost, one of whom is my uncle. We are here to discuss her request."

A man with short-cropped red hair stood up. He wore a lab coat over a sweatsuit, and his fists were clenched at his sides. "You're not going to mention her little attempt at an away mission. This is supposed to be a senior officers' meeting, so Corinne *should* be here instead of me. Unfortunately, she's in the med bay, coming down off a very bad trip. Forget the Outpost. That girl *should* be on bilge duty."

"I don't know what a bil—" Ellis began. Sebastian cut her off with a look.

"Yeah, okay, Morris." Sebastian rubbed his temples, looking frustrated. "I hear you. I'd like to knock down a few of our bigger problems before we work our way to petty retribution."

The red-haired scientist grumbled about it not being petty but raised no further objections. Sebastian, Ellis was beginning to realize, was not a captain in the traditional sense. This was not a military outfit with an ironclad chain of command. It wasn't a commune either, but Sebastian couldn't impose his will on these people without buy-in. Maybe it wasn't he Ellis had to convince.

"Ellis, we need your help," Sebastian announced. It was so sudden and firm that she was taken aback.

"Oh, no." Seb's first mate Val, the small woman who'd driven the other Zodiac, slammed her fist on the table. "Now's not a good time, Cap."

"It's as good a time as any. I'm telling her. If someone wants to challenge me for the hat, You have six seconds, and then I'm telling her."

"Telling me what?" Ellis demanded, but no one answered. Everyone in the room was dead quiet for another five seconds. What did he mean by asking someone to challenge him for the hat? Did he mean the captaincy? She'd nail down their chain of command later.

When Sebastian was sure that no one would challenge him, he pulled down a projector screen. Val plunked a laptop on the table and typed something that made the screen flicker.

"You've spent a few days with us, Ellis," Sebastian continued. "You've toured the ship. You've broken bread with us."

"Waffles, technically," Ellis corrected.

"You've attempted to commandeer our resources," Sebastian added.

"It is an emergency," Ellis protested.

"So you said, and I'm inclined to believe you. But as much as you've learned so far, we haven't told you about our current mission. As part of our everyday work, we track powerful objects."

"Like, weapons?" Ellis asked.

"Sometimes. We've dissolved a lot of unexploded ordinance left over from various wars. But we don't just track bombs or bioweapons. We track computer programs as well. Artificial intelligence systems—that kind of thing."

"You're making it boring, Seb." Val shook her head. "Get to the part everyone wants to hear."

"I'm more excited about convection ovens than a stupid

magic ring," Rami muttered, leaning against the island that separated the mess from the kitchen.

"What magic ring?" Ellis asked.

Sebastian cast an annoyed glance at Rami, who had stolen his big reveal. "In addition to weapons and such, we track magical objects."

Ellis' eyes widened.

"Powerful magical objects can be used as weapons," Val remarked.

"And uranium can fuel a power plant as well as a bomb," Sebastian stated. "Show her."

Val pressed a button, and an image appeared on the screen.

The ring filled the screen. Ellis stared, realizing she was looking at a video rather than a still image. The ring was made of dark metal and featured a single stone—a black pearl restrained by delicate prongs. Shadow magic swirled across the lustrous surface like ocean currents, slow but powerful.

"Where do you keep it?" Ellis asked, staring at the ring. It must take up a huge amount of space on the ship.

"It's not true to scale." Val struggled to conceal her mocking grin.

Sebastian set a small box on the table. Ellis blinked. "Oh."

Ellis opened the box, embarrassed by her mistake. The ring within looked like the one on the screen, but she couldn't see the swirling shadow magic.

"It's different," Ellis muttered uncertainly. "What happened to the magic?"

Sebastian frowned.

"She can't see it." Val sounded uneasy, but there was a whiff of "Gotcha." Val turned to Ellis. "We have special lenses for the non-magical crew. That video was taken with one such lens."

"Is she right? You're not a shadow mage?" Sebastian asked. "That's impossible. We've seen you use your powers a thousand times."

Ellis was oscillating between truth and a plausible-sounding lie when the guard to her left said, "She hasn't used any magic since coming on board. Not even during the escape attempt."

"Shit!" Sebastian exclaimed.

"I told you," Val hissed at him. "You've gone and told her all our secrets for no reason."

"No way." Sebastian shook his head. "The intel from LA was unambiguous. The bank robbery, for instance."

Ellis gripped the edge of the table tightly. Sebastian needed her for something that required shadow magic. She was sure of it. "What does all this have to do with the ring?"

"No!" Val cut in. "If she can't do this, there's no point in telling her more."

Sebastian hesitated, then shook his head. "Our grandmother left home to look for that ring. We're not sure what information she was following, although we think it came from an ancient drow scroll. Whatever it was, it was urgent enough to send her up to explore the surface."

"*She* found the ring?" Ellis asked, running her finger over the metal. It was cool to the touch. More than cool, and more than hard metal. An invisible barrier rose when Ellis' skin brushed it. She shivered and withdrew her hand.

"*We* found the ring," Val corrected.

"We finished what Elandra started," Sebastian admonished. "Before she died, my mother told me what Elandra had said to her. Elandra thought the ring could only be worn by someone with both drow and human ancestry."

Now Ellis understood. The crew of the *Violet Eel* had stumbled on an artifact that was full to bursting with power and maybe dangerous because of it.

"You need a guinea pig, don't you? You don't want to risk anyone on your crew, so you want me to test it."

Sebastian frowned, and Val looked at Ellis with loathing. "I told you it can't be her, Seb. She doesn't get it."

"Get what?" Ellis asked.

"The captain would never ask anyone to do his dirty work for him," Val shot back.

"I can't access the power in the ring. When I put it on… it's hard to describe, but it feels like I'm jogging into a brick wall. It's not horrible, but there's nowhere to go."

"We've all tried it," Peri explained. "Everyone with a mixed background."

"And everyone *without* a mixed background." Rami waggled his fingers.

"*You've got* fat *fingers,*" Val shouted, a friendly jab.

The senior officers traded barbs for a minute before Sebastian hushed them. "I wanted you to have a positive experience on this ship. I wanted you to ask to join the crew after you saw us work together and understood our mission."

"Instead, you're using my father's life to coerce me," Ellis growled. "What is the ring supposed to do?"

There was a long pause. "We don't know," Sebastian admitted.

"If it gives me a godlike power, what's to stop me from sinking your ship and flying back to Los Angeles on my own?"

"She makes a great point, Seb." Val wore an expression between a grin and a sneer.

"I know enough about you to know you wouldn't do that," Sebastian told Ellis. "Well, the sinking the ship part, anyway. I hope if you developed godlike omnipotence, you'd use it to understand my sincerity."

"If I try the ring on, you'll let me take the treatment to my dad?" Ellis asked.

Sebastian nodded. "I will, yes. However, it almost certainly requires a shadow magic user. If our intel is wrong, there's no shame in it. I'm not a shadow mage either."

His casual tone shocked Ellis. No hint of embarrassment. It was like he was telling her his blood type. Ellis couldn't imagine feeling that way. She would have to tell Sebastian the truth, and her face was already turning red.

"I've…had some difficulties," Ellis explained. Before she realized what she was doing, she spilled her history with shadow magic from her early vigilante work in Los Angeles to her first encounter with the DRI to her eventual imprisonment and the damage done by the organization's lightsilk. She glossed over the worst bits, but when she finished, the senior officers looked horrified.

She looked at the ship's doctor, a spark of hope igniting. He looked like Val, and she wondered if they were siblings. "Have you run across this before? Can you do anything to help?" Hope welled.

The doctor mulled that, then shook his head. "I'm sorry,

but I don't know of any potions or procedures that would restore your powers. I'm happy to check our archives, but I'm not optimistic."

Sebastian nodded. "When we need to, we suppress shadow magic…" His voice trailed off after a hard look from Val. "We have a few ways of doing it, but they're nothing like what you describe. They've never changed someone's shadow magic abilities long-term."

Ellis stood up. "Maybe it will be pointless, but I'll try to use the ring." She shivered as she ran a finger around the interior. "If you help my dad, I'll do whatever you want."

CHAPTER SIX

The soldier Charlie had dubbed Good Cop put a Starbucks coffee and a chicken sandwich in front of him. He was about the same height and build as Charlie, which he guessed was meant to put him at ease. Bad Cop had six inches and forty pounds on him, plus a vicious scar running down the center of his face that had missed his eye by a millimeter but taken out a chunk of his nose.

Good Cop had given Charlie a fake name the first time they met, but neither remembered it. Against his better judgment, Charlie liked the bluff, good-natured soldier. That was the point. The man had a sixth sense for Charlie's favorite snacks and never got ruffled.

"Thank you for the food and coffee. I'd like to see my lawyer now," Charlie said after taking a long sip. He assessed the sandwich for a clue as to his location. Green peppers for New Mexico? Pimento cheese for the South? Avocado for California? *You can get avocados in Alaska, dummy.* Charlie hoped he wasn't in Alaska.

"Look, Charlie, I want to help you. I do," Good Cop

insisted. Charlie snorted, which elicited a rare frown. Unfortunately, it also sent coffee up his nose. Good Cop waited until he was done coughing. "Help me out, man. My bosses are up my ass. If you can tell me *anything* new..."

"Okay," Charlie said. When Good Cop gave him a friendly smile, he drawled, *"Yo quiero un abogado."*

"You want an avocado?" Good Cop grinned.

Charlie thought he was joking, although if Good Cop didn't know the word for "lawyer" in Spanish, they probably weren't in Southern California. That wasn't much to go on. Charlie sipped the coffee again.

"You got everything you need, man? I can get you more blankets. Maybe a book or two."

"Sure. I'd appreciate that," Charlie agreed.

"All right, but you gotta give me *something,* Charlie," Good Cop repeated.

Charlie finished his coffee in slow sips. His interrogator was getting frustrated. Crumpling the empty cup in one fist, Charlie continued, "I get it, man. Talking to a blank wall is no fun. If you're bored, you and Scarface can switch roles." He nodded at the two-way mirror, which Good Cop's mean-mugging partner was almost certainly standing behind. "I'd like to see him play nice. That would be entertaining. You think he knows any jokes?"

The soldier stood up, collected Charlie's plate and the crumpled cup, walked to the door, and knocked on it twice. It sprang open. "Remember that I tried to help you," Good Cop said ominously.

Uh-oh. Playtime might be over.

Charlie wondered for the umpteenth time if he should disappear and try to find a way out of the room. Shadow magic was the ultimate get-out-of-jail-free card, but he didn't want to be careless with it. He had Percy and Rose to think about, for one. His feelings toward Mikhail were less charitable, but he didn't want to get the kid murdered.

If he played his hand, he wanted to make it count. These weren't regular troops. They were Special Ops of some kind, so they might know about shadow magic. Hell, the building might be surrounded by a lightsilk net, so he would play along for the time being.

So far, his imprisonment had been boring but not dangerous. A medic had treated the burns on his face and cleaned his wrists, and Bad Cop hadn't hurt him. Bad Cop hadn't even threatened to hurt him. He had only served Charlie terrible powdered coffee and described in detail his plan to have Charlie charged with various counts of terrorism and treason for breaking into the Chiaro Institute, all of which were capital crimes.

Bad Cop enjoyed describing the process of lethal injection. Good Cop was increasingly frustrated by Charlie's polite, repetitive requests for a lawyer, but Bad Cop enjoyed them, growing increasingly convinced that Charlie would be thrown under a legal steamroller.

When the door to the interrogation room re-opened, Charlie steeled himself for another round of threats.

"Lawyer," he told the empty room.

Arden Chan sat down in front of him. "Harvard Law, class of 2002. Top of my class, in fact."

Charlie made a startled noise before pulling himself together. Finally, help had arrived. "Senator, I'm glad to see you, although I doubt you've stooped to indigent criminal defense."

"Indigent? Come on, Charlie. I've seen your bank accounts."

Hey, I've been living in a cave. "If you're here to spring me, I'm happy to drum up a retainer." His heart sank as her expression hardened. The hot water he was in was about to boil over. He was glad he'd kept the lid on his shadow magic. "Are you here with a carrot or a stick?"

"I'm here to find out who broke into the Chiaro Institute," Senator Chan replied. "I am here to ask you, as a loyal citizen of the United States, to tell me what you know."

"What's the Chiaro Institute?" Charlie asked with a blank face.

Chan sighed. "Unlike the men you've been speaking to, I don't have unlimited time. I've got the President breathing down my neck, and I need answers sooner rather than later."

"Tell POTUS I'll be happy to help him out after I see my lawyer."

Chan's voice softened. "Look, Charlie. I know *you* didn't break into the institute. No one we picked up did. You couldn't have. That intrusion required a particular set of skills that we're both familiar with."

More than you know, Senator. "I can't help you."

"That's too bad. If you can't help us, things will get quite a bit less comfortable."

Her face went hard, and Charlie shivered.

CHAPTER SEVEN

"What am I supposed to *do* with the ring?" Ellis asked. She had the black metal band in her palm.

"Put it on," Sebastian offered.

"Then what?"

"See what happens," Val added cheerfully, sounding like she hoped it would be painful.

Ellis turned it around a few times, then slipped it onto her ring finger. The band was cool at first and got colder. Her body shook as icy tendrils wrapped around her skin like the thinnest spiderwebs. She held out her hands, desperate to see what it was that was enveloping her. Not exactly shadow magic. Something...different.

Maybe this is how it's supposed to feel. Ellis straightened. The ring was having no visible effect on her skin, but she could feel those spiderweb strands of cold on her arms and legs and torso. There was something within the ring, but Ellis couldn't access it. She was missing a piece of the puzzle.

The web tightened, pressing in. She was like a balloon

squeezed in a vise, ready to pop but with nowhere for the air to go. If she could access her shadow magic, she could make sense of it, but it was gone, and the ice web around her was grasping for that empty place.

Ellis ripped the ring off with a gasp. The icy spiderweb fell away, and the grasping fingers released her back into the mess hall. She was shivering, although the people around her didn't seem concerned.

"Leave it on for a second or two," Val grumbled.

"Why?" Ellis tossed the ring back into the case, half-expecting her finger to be frozen.

Her alarm registered with Val, who asked, "What happened?"

"I don't think I can help," Ellis stated.

"Something happened, didn't it?" Sebastian asked.

"Nothing good," Ellis replied.

The captain rushed forward and grabbed Ellis' arm but quickly snatched his hand away. "You're freezing. What happened? Explain it to me."

Ellis told him about the sensation of icy fingers grasping for a void. The officers around her exchanged looks. Val was annoyed. Rami was bemused. The captain seemed triumphant.

"You did it. I know you did. Try it again."

"Her teeth are chattering," Rami admonished. "At least let me get her some tea."

Ellis shook her head. "It won't work until I get my shadow magic back. I can feel it. This is...a different kind of magic. It's cold. It's half of a whole. The ring needs something I haven't got."

Shit. Would Sebastian refuse to treat her dad now?

"There might be a way. One of my friends at the Homestead? She created a potion that helped me use shadow magic. She's very good. The best, maybe. If anyone can help me, it's her." Could Trissa develop a new potion in time to save Connor, Ilva, and Ulivi?

Sebastian was watching her.

"If you deliver the cure to my dad, I'll track Trissa down," Ellis offered.

Sebastian sighed. "I want your word. On Elandra's honor."

Ellis sucked in her breath. That was an oath she took seriously. She had wanted to deliver the cure to her father herself, but that wasn't the important thing. Walking over, she stuck out her hand. "You have it. You have my personal word on Nan's honor."

"How do you know her word is *worth* anything?" Val sounded annoyed.

Sebastian grinned. "Family resemblance." He took Ellis' hand, and they shook.

"I'm not sure what kind of reception I'll get at the Homestead," Ellis continued. "But they need to know the truth about Lola. She might still have co-conspirators there. I-I think I should go alone."

There was a disturbance at the back of the room as the door opened. Jerel, the medic, rushed in.

"Sorry to interrupt," he began breathlessly, "But Claire Burton just woke up."

Ellis didn't wait for Captain Sebastian to dismiss her. She pushed past one of the big men who tried to get in her way.

"Let her go," Sebastian called.

Ellis sprinted down the hall to the nearest staircase, walls flashing by. Someone shouted behind her, but she ignored them and burst through the medical bay's doors.

"*Mom!*" Ellis shouted, and Claire looked up. She was very pale, but her face brightened at the sight of Ellis.

Claire was attached to too many tubes for Ellis to hug her, so she settled for squeezing her leg again. "How do you feel?"

"Like I've been keelhauled under a cruise liner," Claire replied glumly.

"You look..."

"I look like shit. It's fine. I'll get better. Apparently."

Jerel burst in, followed by the chief physician.

"Can she leave with me? When will she be well enough to travel?" Ellis asked.

"You should talk to Sebastian about that," Dr. Moray told her.

As it turned out, the captain was right behind her, so she turned around. "I want to take Mom with me."

Sebastian's face was grim. "Ellis, as you can imagine, we've been speaking to Mirelle about your mother's role at the DRI and her collaboration with Klimova."

Claire's body lost its energy. She slumped on her pillow, reflexively closing her eyes. "The chickens have come home to roost, huh?"

"Do you really wish to advocate for her after she joined the research team of a woman who wanted to kill the world?" Sebastian asked.

"They kidnapped me! She didn't have a choice!" Ellis exclaimed.

Sebastian's voice was hard when he spoke. "*Everyone* has a choice."

"If it's all the same to you, Ellis, I'd rather stay here," Claire offered softly.

"Your mother has significant insights about drow physiology to share," Sebastian explained.

"No, she's done with that. The DRI era is over." Her mother's research formed a dark, unspoken chasm between them.

"Maybe I can atone a little," Claire suggested. "Besides, the sea air is good for me."

"If you'd like to join the science team, you can start by telling me about *this.*" Sebastian retrieved the test tube containing Connor's cure.

"It's a phage tailored to Ellis' father's illness," she replied immediately.

"Give the doc the details, and he'll pass them along," Sebastian told Claire. "If you'll excuse me, I have to get back to the bridge. We'll dock in Long Beach in three hours."

CHAPTER EIGHT

Ellis drove a rented Honda along the highway. Sebastian had deemed the motorcycle she wanted "operationally unnecessary." *That's the fun of a motorcycle.* He'd wanted to send someone with her, but Ellis had refused to show anyone else the main entrance to the drow Homestead.

She wondered if Charlie's body was still there. Returning it to the surface would have raised questions. Maybe they had held a funeral and dropped it into the pit of the ancestors. She pulled the car off the road a half-mile from the turnoff and walked from there, not wanting to mark the entrance.

She had much to tell her people. Pushing through the undergrowth, she reached the mouth of the cave. She'd always had mixed feelings about homecomings, but now that Charlie was gone, she just felt numb. The cavern narrowed to a tall break in the rock just wide enough for a single body. Behind it, guards murmured in low voices.

"Hello? It's me," she called in a low voice, not eager to take an arrow to the throat.

She still couldn't see the guards, but they went silent. Then one of them said, "Call the rangers and get the unit here." Someone ran, and a figure stepped into the narrow gap guarding the entrance. Flashes of purple blocked the cavern beyond.

Rage gripped Ellis' heart when she saw who it was. Her anger squeezed her until a thin layer of red washed over her vision.

Lola.

She smiled at Ellis, a knowing, cold expression that crossed the gap between them as hard and fast as a rock-fall. After a moment, however, the wicked smile changed. The bottom lip trembled, and Lola languidly rearranged her expression into a facsimile of fear.

"Please don't hurt me!" Lola cried, making her voice shake.

Ellis fumed. She had seen Lola afraid, but this was phony. She would not fall for it. She ran forward until her hands made a satisfying contact with the base of Lola's neck. Together, they tumbled to the ground. Ellis swung on top, grip tightening.

"Lola!" the guard screamed, and the air at Ellis' back chilled.

"Don't. It's too dangerous." Lola's voice came out in a squeak. Presumably, the other guard had been preparing to use defensive shadow magic. Ellis' guts roiled, but she wrapped her fingers tighter.

Then strong hands pulled her away from the purple-skinned woman who had killed Charlie Morrissey. Ellis clawed at the hands, but the guard pulling her back was stronger, and she barely managed to scratch him.

"Let me go!" Ellis screamed. "She's a traitor!"

She kicked at Lola, who dodged her and slipped to the back, then helped the drow guard secure Ellis' wrists. Lola had been managing an out-of-control brother for months, so she was at least as strong as Ellis. Ellis couldn't free herself without snapping her arm bones.

As she tried to struggle free, a knot of people sprinted up from the bowels of the Homestead, led by Priya. As they came into hearing distance, Lola leaned forward, breath hot on Ellis' earlobe. "You should have heard the way Charlie cried under all those rocks. His blood washed the Homestead clean again," she whispered just loud enough for Ellis to hear.

Then she released Ellis' wrists. It was like uncaging a wild animal. Lola's words bit into her soul and she spun, a ball of burning violence, and slammed Lola against the nearest wall. The drow woman went limp in her arms.

"Help!" Lola cried. Ellis tightened her hands, desperate to push those stupid words out of the woman's throat. Lola swayed like a rag doll in her grasp. Why wasn't she fighting back? Her feigned helplessness stoked Ellis' fury, and she delivered sharp blows to Lola's guts before wrapping her hands back around that slender purple neck, pressing all the breath out. Lola had killed Charlie, and she had been willing to kill all the other humans on Earth. She didn't deserve mercy.

Someone shouted, and dust exploded in front of Ellis' face. She blinked away the pungent fungal powder, but it filled her eyes again the next time she breathed. Her hands were losing their grip, and she struggled to remember what she was doing. As the dust went up Ellis' nose, her vision gently detached from reality. She was unmoored for a moment. Before she collapsed, she saw Lola smirking in triumph.

Ellis' last thought as she sank into darkness was that she had walked into a trap.

CHAPTER NINE

From his conversations with the surrounding wildlife on their long drive to their current location, Percy guessed that he was being held prisoner in the great flat expanse that divided California from Nevada. He'd kept up solid communication with a flock of birds throughout the ride, but after they'd been led stumbling into a building and then an elevator, he'd lost contact.

Based on the length of the elevator ride, they were deep underground, and he'd even lost contact with the underground insects. He tried to reassure himself with a reminder that there was life everywhere, even in the Atacama desert and the deep marine trenches.

He was attempting to build a friendship with a cockroach that sometimes wandered into his small cell by throwing crumbs of the food they brought him on the ground near the nest. However, the guards cleaned and searched his cell whenever he went to the interrogation room, and it was always impeccable when he returned. The cockroach's mind was too small and strange for him to establish meaningful communication.

Percy wished he could still talk to Mariner. Albatrosses had impressive endurance, but a bird couldn't beat a gas-powered car in a long-distance race, and she'd fallen away in the middle of the desert.

He'd make new contacts sooner or later. No environment would stay sterile forever. Still, animal chatter was different from human chatter, and he missed his rich community of friends. The only people he talked to now were the guards. And Senator Chan, who had appeared in the interrogation room this morning.

"You're slippery, Percy," Chan began. "We haven't found your digital footprints anywhere. Regular web. Dark web. Nothing. That means you're either a hermit or a pro. My money is on pro since hermits rarely become bank robbers."

Percy fiddled with the hem of the gray t-shirt they had given him to wear. Not his style at all. He let Chan's words wash over him, waiting to see if she would give away any information.

"Look, Percy. If you won't help yourself, help your friends," Chan urged. At that, Percy perked up. "We *know* none of you broke into Chiaro, but unless you tell us who did, we're going to be stuck in this cycle. You four are more obstinate than my teenage children, and we can't run on this hamster wheel forever."

Percy raised his eyebrows. "That's the point of a hamster wheel, ma'am."

Chan made an unsupportive noise. "I can't keep wasting

government resources, so I'll liven things up with a deadline. Unless we get actionable information about the Chiaro break-in in the next three days, all four of you will be transferred to a black site. Do you understand what that means?

"You go in, and you don't come out," Percy replied.

"Exactly. Look, Percy…" Senator Chan said his name too often. All his interrogators did. It was one of their tricks, and it reminded him to stay on his guard. "We're not the bad guys here."

"The black site you're threatening me with is a real white-hat heroic place, huh?"

She frowned. "Sometimes lesser evils serve the greater good. The Chiaro Institute's research would be *extremely* dangerous in the wrong hands."

"We agree on one thing, but we're in conflict about whose hands are *wrong.*"

"If you won't try to save yourself, perhaps you'll try to save your friends. Don't you want to help Rose?" Chan asked.

"Not Charlie?" Percy asked. "He's worth less 'cuz he's a man?"

This was a gamble. Percy cared about all his friends, but Chan had been smart to threaten Rose. He had never guessed he could connect with a human as strongly as he could with an animal. Maybe it was her wild side. Rose understood and embraced her primal instincts. Her choice of careers, which he tried to be neutral about, took advantage of those strengths. Caging someone like that was a crime against nature.

Three days wouldn't be enough to escape. He couldn't see a way through the problem, but Chan had given him a very clear deadline, and there was no sense in rushing straight to failure. He'd have to try something. If he could get to Charlie, they might be able to formulate a plan. His animal telepathy was powerful when combined with Charlie's newfound shadow magic.

Chan left, and two soldiers took Percy back to his cell. The floor was spotless, and the smell of bleach irritated his nose. No sign of the cockroach under the bed or in the room's crevices. Maybe the chemicals had gotten to it.

Percy lay down on the cell's hard cot, closed his eyes, and breathed deeply. Not to sleep but to ground himself. He needed more information before he made a decision, and stretching his animal telepathy to the maximum was the only way he could think of to improve his understanding.

He knew he was underground. The surroundings weren't as dead near the surface. There were worms and bugs in the soil and small mammals everywhere. He wasn't sure how deep he was, though. Making an effort to find out, he stretched his awareness overhead, focusing on a narrow circle of ceiling above him and pushing his powers to their limit. Under this strain, his head ached. *It'll be worth it if I find something.*

Nothing was what he felt first. A big fat hole of dead rock, a vertical column of emptiness. Percy pushed, ignoring the blade of pain pressing into his brain stem. *How deep am I?* His awareness moved up through the dead zone. It was eerie and despairing, and he fought the urge to retreat and pressed on. It couldn't be dead forever unless they were somewhere really weird, like a nuclear silo. The

United States military had better things to do with its nuclear silos than prisoner detention.

He rose through the column, and just as he was about to give up, something wiggled.

Charlie sighed in relief. There was a mind above him. Barely a blip, but it was there.

Hello, he sent.

The mind above him barely reacted. Percy pushed it, attempting to glean information.

A worm. He sighed in frustration. A worm couldn't help him get out of military custody. A worm couldn't deliver a message to anyone who *could* help. It was comforting, that brush with life and vitality, but that was all.

Percy tried to push further but couldn't. Maybe with training and concerted effort, it would be possible, but he didn't have the time. He had three days.

The next day, he banged on his door, and when a soldier came, he asked for Senator Chan. The guard made no promises, but three hours later, they retrieved him from his cell.

"I hope you haven't cost the American taxpayers an unnecessary helicopter ride," she said, sliding a large, hot mocha over to him. "It's got oat milk."

Percy understood how to train a dog using positive rewards. "Thank you," he replied, but he didn't touch it. She waited patiently, sipping her own coffee. There was a ballpoint pen and a yellow legal pad in front of her.

"I'm here to make a deal," he began.

She smiled, pushing the pen and legal pad toward him. "We need names, dates, places, everything. Take your time."

He pushed the pad back toward her, and she frowned. "I'm not here for that kind of deal."

"That's the only deal there is," Chan retorted.

"You're gonna change your mind on that," Percy stated.

Her eyes widened at his confidence. "Oh?"

"I'm an animal psychic," Percy told her without preamble.

He wasn't surprised by her patronizing smile. So few people in his life had believed him when he said it that he'd had it printed on business cards without worrying about the consequences.

The pen and paper slid back toward him. "You can joke all you like, Percy, but you know what we need."

"It's not a joke. It's a real thing."

"Mmm."

"Why'd you think my brother was keepin' all those creatures at the DRI?" Percy asked.

"Research."

"True but incomplete."

"Why should I believe you?"

"Why should you believe someone who tells you they can turn invisible and put a hole through a wall with their mind?" Percy asked. "Because it's true. That's why."

Chan tapped her fingernail on the table, and her expression shifted into grudging acknowledgment. "What is your deal? You're going to convince my cat to stop scratching the furniture?"

"I'd be happy to have a conversation with him, but cats are independent creatures with their own motivations. I was thinking more along the lines of allowing Uncle Sam to put my brain under a microscope."

Chan's eyebrows rose.

"Not literally, I hope. Least not 'til I've died a natural death after a long, productive life. But I'd cooperate with your research. That's the deal. I stay and let you study my powers, and you set the others free."

"If you can prove what you're saying is true, I'll consider it."

Percy beamed. "Wonderful. I know you haven't got any dogs in this place, but maybe you do up top? Guard dogs? Local canine units? Something like that?"

Senator Chan was very still. "Who told you we were underground?"

"No one told me. I can just tell. If we were up top, there'd be birds."

She searched his face for a lie.

"Now, you go rustle up a dog, and you'll see I'm telling the truth."

Chan rapped once on the door. "Have we got any K-9 units on the property?" she asked. The soldier looked surprised but said he knew of one. Chan nodded and gave him clipped instructions. "All right, Mr. Rawlings. You've got your test."

CHAPTER TEN

Ellis woke up in one of the small lightsilk-lined rooms that were the closest thing the Homestead had to a jail rather than in the infirmary. Two drow men she only vaguely recognized were stationed outside. They barred her exit when she tried to leave and refused to talk to her, although they brought her food at regular intervals.

It was boring. Ellis broke up the intervals between meals with pushups and naps. Finally, she resorted to counting the glowing lichen spots on the ceiling. She had reached three hundred and twelve when someone threw aside the curtain across the door.

It was Lola. Ellis blinked when she saw what the young drow was wearing. "Does Katya know you stole her speakers' robes?"

"Katya recently retired," Lola stated.

Ellis felt like the floor had tilted forty-five degrees. "What do you mean, *retired*?"

"The drow weren't happy with the way things have

changed." Lola's voice was threatening. "Katya and the others understood that and stood down."

"You organized a coup," Ellis whispered.

Lola fumbled with the long metal staff Katya had held so effortlessly. "Changes in leadership are healthy. The Homestead needed a fresh young perspective."

The metal staff hit the wall of the cavern when she gestured with it. Her sleeves, embroidered with swirling patterns in jewel tones, draped awkwardly over her long purple fingers. Lola clearly hadn't found the time to have them hemmed.

"Your robes don't fit," Ellis observed pointedly.

Lola narrowed her eyes. "You're not in a position to criticize me." She self-consciously pushed the sleeve up.

"Do the elders know you murdered Rollo?" Ellis asked, going on the offensive. "Does the rest of the Homestead know?"

"Oh, please. You can stop projecting now. Everyone knows you were behind the plot to kill Rollo and then the other leaders. We're still not sure who shot the arrow, but several of your collaborators were detained. I have every confidence that one of them will confess."

Ellis had seriously misjudged this situation. So much for her vision of going into the Homestead and dragging Lola before the elder council. There *was* no elder council now. And what did Lola mean by her "collaborators?"

"I want to see Landon," Ellis insisted. He would know that Lola was lying. He'd be able to tell her the truth.

"So you can get your stories straight? Hah. Not likely. Don't worry. He's being held in a safe place, along with his little girlfriend. She was relieved of her duties in the infirmary. Participating in a murder plot was a clear violation of her healer's oath."

"You can't do this!" Ellis exclaimed.

Lola looked around, feigning surprise. "Really? That's news to me. We're having an all-meet later today, and your fate will be sealed."

"This is my home," Ellis insisted. "You can't exile me."

"Exile? I wasn't thinking of that. You've got a lot of friends on the outside, and you're tricky. Erasing your memory is more appropriate. Give you a nice clean slate. The good news is, without their tiring political responsibilities, the former elders have more energy to focus on the blank-out spell."

Lola's eyes were bright when she said it, and the rock arch framing her seemed to fall away into darkness. Ellis was terrified and might have been paralyzed if she hadn't had burning anger to animate her body.

"So, that's the plan? Kill Charlie and wipe my memory of your crimes?"

"That would be letting you off too lightly," Lola countered. "Your sins started long before the past few months. They started when you began sneaking off to Los Angeles."

That had been years ago. Surely Lola wasn't suggesting wiping out years of her memories.

"If I hadn't started 'sneaking off to Los Angeles,' Irving would still be in a cage," Ellis growled.

Lola's face looked like it had been carved from amethyst. She was beyond logic or regret.

"When is my hearing?" Ellis demanded. She was accused of serious crimes, and she had the right to speak on her own behalf before her people. Even if they wouldn't help her, she could warn them about Lola. A few would believe her.

"I see no reason to subject my people to your outsider poison," Lola replied. "A hearing won't be necessary."

Ellis was furious. How had Lola poisoned the Homestead and dissolved so much of their tradition so quickly? The elders were old, and what was happening now was new.

"How did you escape the yacht?" Ellis asked. "I saw the wreckage. Seb...the boats looked for survivors for hours."

"I could ask you the same question, and I will. As for my escape, I stayed invisible in the water and snuck aboard a Navy search and rescue ship. It docked in Long Beach a day later. I had just enough juice in my medallion to make it home."

Ellis cursed. It hadn't occurred to her that someone might actively try to avoid Sebastian's rescue team. Getting out must have been quite a feat. A reminder to never underestimate the woman.

"Irving has been through enough. He doesn't need his sister orchestrating a coup," Ellis continued, making a play for Lola's sense of decency. Whatever her other flaws, Lola cared deeply for her brother.

"Irving needs his fellow drow," Lola shot back. "He doesn't need the Outpost, and he *really* doesn't need humans. Having you back to how you were before you started all this nonsense will be good for him. Maybe after I rewind you, I'll become your friend. You could be a valuable ally."

It was such an absurd suggestion that Ellis snorted. "Landon won't let you get away with this. He'll tell everyone the truth about who you are. Los Angeles made us closer, as did the Outpost. We barely spoke before. If you think Landon will welcome having our relationship ripped away, you're stupider than you seem."

Lola hesitated. Then her terrible forward momentum flattened her doubts. "Maybe we'll wipe his memory, too."

"*What!* No! He doesn't know you murdered Rollo," Ellis protested.

Lola's face looked softer, but her eyes were still terrible. "It might be good for him to forget about the DRI. Not a punishment, but therapy. If it works, maybe…"

Even though her voice trailed off, the thought hit the target. Ellis wondered if a brain-wipe would cure her brother's trauma. "You're using me as a lab rat," Ellis said when realization dawned. "You want to help Irving, so you're going to wipe my memory and maybe my brother's so the elders can perfect the spell."

She could tell from Lola's expression that she was right on the money. After a moment, Lola shook her head.

"I'm doing what's best for my people," Lola stated to convince herself.

Ellis could tell that she wouldn't get any further today. "I'm hungry. Did you bring food?"

Lola tossed a tunnel bar wrapped in silk on the foot of Ellis' bed and left without another word.

CHAPTER ELEVEN

Sebastian Altamont wanted to pace, but his cabin wasn't big enough. Ellis' three missed check-ins had made him antsy, and his claustrophobic quarters didn't help. Sometimes, shipboard living wasn't ideal.

The captain's cabin was luxurious compared to the crew's quarters. However, the only real luxury on a working ship was privacy. He could go out and pace on the deck if he wanted to, but that would invite the crew to bring him problems. He was already confronting his primary problem.

Had she disappeared of her own volition? Maybe Ellis hadn't wanted to wield her long-lost cousin's magic ring and had taken the opportunity to escape. She had given her word, but had he put too much stock in that? If her word was no good, she wasn't who they needed anyway.

His toe slammed into the wall, sending a shock of pain up his leg. Sebastian forced himself to be still, but that only lasted for a few minutes. He decided he would walk off his nerves on the way to the lab.

The science department was understaffed. Ellis' hallucinogenic spray had been effective. Clever, too. As promised, Corinne hadn't been harmed, but she was still upset by the experience, and he'd given her a few days of shore leave. People in Los Angeles paid a lot of money for that kind of psychedelic journey, but she had not experienced it as either enjoyable or revealing.

He ran into Morris at the door. As usual, the scientist's clothes were covered in mustard stains. His lab coat was clean, at least.

"Captain! I was just coming to see you. I've cleared that test tube Ellis Burton was trying to sneak off the boat. It's not a threat unless you're a gram-negative bacteria."

"So, it is what she said?" Sebastian asked. He was desperately hoping the answer was yes. The rest of his family was dead, and he wasn't eager to lose a new cousin.

"I can't confirm that the cure will work," the doctor equivocated. "There's only one way to know that, but it's not contagious. Won't hurt anyone else."

"Thank you." Sebastian was unable to conceal his relief. He went to find Val. It was time to put together an away team.

She wasn't thrilled about the mission. No surprise there. Val was fiercely loyal to *Violet Eel*'s crew and fiercely antagonistic to everyone else. It made her a terrific first officer, and it usually served his goals. Val took care of the crew, and the crew took care of the mission. But sometimes, convincing her to care about people outside of their immediate circle felt like pulling teeth.

When *Violet Eel* recruited new crew members, she was adversarial until her switch flipped when they signed their paperwork. The rapid-fire personality change made some newbies uneasy.

She was dead set against helping Ellis Burton, but she got in line eventually. Once she got going, she was fast and efficient, and in less than twelve hours, they were in a van headed to Hollywood.

He'd almost left her on the ship, but he wanted his A-team, so here she was, staring out the passenger's seat window at the Bromeliad.

"We're raiding a fancy ladies' social club, huh? What are we gonna do, pillage their Goop subscriptions?" Val asked. She knew about the Outpost in the basement as well as he did, but she was upset that they were on the mission and was fighting him at every turn.

Sebastian ignored the quip about the Bromeliad, wondering if he should have brought Claire instead. That would have been its own can of worms, though. Unlike Val or even Ellis, Claire was dangerous, but she'd been willing to share information about the Outpost's layout.

This will be easy. We're glorified delivery boys. He patted the test tube in his pocket and checked his appearance in the rearview mirror a final time.

Sebastian could go out in public without makeup if he needed to. The purple splotches on his face read as birthmarks to most people—port wine stains. Today, though, he'd put on concealer and big sunglasses. They didn't need to draw any extra attention.

"How does the radio sound?" he asked.

His young comms officer Ollie pulled his headphones off. "It's quiet." He frowned.

"Something wrong?" Sebastian asked.

"I don't know. Given what Claire told us, I expected to pick up more security feeds. I thought I'd pick up *something, b*ut it's totally dead below ground level."

"Okay. What does that mean?"

"I don't know. It's...weird."

"Hmm." Sebastian didn't like weird. He liked things to be on schedule, on budget, and well-understood. He had them all check their earpieces just to be safe. Then, they climbed out of the van.

Everyone on this mission was, or at least looked, human. There was only one shadow mage in their number, a compact young half-drow named Zelda who stayed cool under pressure. The rest of them carried hush puppies and cloakers that were spheres instead of cylinders and would give them ten minutes of invisibility if they needed it.

For the moment, they used neither. Instead, they simply walked into the lobby. Claire said that the Bromeliad was accustomed to unusual guests heading straight to the basement, which was technically true. There was no one in the lobby, just leafy plants and silence. A small reception desk in the depths of the room was abandoned.

Sebastian felt uneasy but went and pressed the elevator button. The doors popped open with a ding, and his team stepped inside. Before he could swipe Claire's keycard against the electronic lock, the doors closed, and the elevator began to descend. Sebastian hit the button for Sub-basement Two, but nothing happened.

That was also weird. He tried a few more buttons, but they remained dim, and the elevator didn't slow.

"Something's wrong," Sebastian announced. "Turn your cloakers and hush puppies on."

He reached into his pocket and flicked the switches. Zelda, relying on her powers, reached into the dark corners of the elevator and cast a swift invisibility spell. As Sebastian pulled his hand out of his pocket, he noticed a fisheye lens in a corner of the ceiling—a security cam. The air around him cooled, and he unholstered his sidearm. The crew of the *Violet Eel* rarely used weapons since it was too easy for invisible people to fall to friendly fire. But he was in the lead, and something was very wrong.

They went down to Sub-basement Three before the elevator stopped. He had expected to be met with force, so he was surprised when the doors opened onto a nearly empty hallway.

A small device was stationed just outside the elevator. It looked like a stack of metal boxes on a wheeled platform. Because of his hush puppy, Sebastian failed to hear the series of beeps.

He saw the blinking red light turn solid, but it was too late.

"Get down—" he screamed as the device exploded.

Sparks peppered Sebastian's vision as he dropped to the floor. The hush puppy protected his hearing, and as soft, unfamiliar flecks brushed his skin, he realized he'd been mistaken about the sparks. The bomb hadn't released explosives but *confetti.* The glittering silky scraps floated through the air like snowflakes.

There was movement at his side, and Zelda rolled out into the hallway, screaming in pain. Why had she dropped her invisibility spell?

When he saw the red welts rising on her hands, he thought he understood.

This must be the lightsilk Ellis had told him about. It had sucked out Zelda's magic. Did that mean their cloakers had stopped working?

Sebastian SEAL-crawled forward to pull Zelda back into the elevator, but it was too late. Soldiers clad in familiar silver lightsilk fabric burst out of a doorway ten feet down the hall and ran toward Zelda with a net. Sebastian backed away by instinct, realizing as he did that not a single soldier was looking into the elevator.

"Where the fuck did the rest of them go?" one of the men shouted.

The lightsilk hadn't affected the cloakers. Sebastian and the rest of his team were still invisible. That was interesting.

"Hold," Sebastian ordered before someone surged forward to help Zelda. They needed to be careful to avoid giving away their hand.

While two of the waiting soldiers pressed Zelda to the floor, their leader picked up a walkie-talkie. "We got one of them," he reported. Then, his face darkened. "The other three...disappeared. No, not like that. We hit 'em good with the confetti. I don't know, either. Yes, Senator. Okay, Senator."

Senator? Sebastian filed that tidbit away for later.

The soldier looked like he was about to leave, but then he paused, eyes fixed on the elevator. After a moment, he twitched his fingers at the doors.

"Clear it, boys."

"But sir, if an MEC was in there—"

"Just *do* it!"

Shit. Two young, nervous-looking soldiers surged forward.

"Get down," Sebastian barked as the soldiers crossed the threshold of his hush puppy. As he dove to the floor, the shifting envelope ruffled the hair on his neck.

"Oh, shit!" the kid said as Sebastian flipped onto his back. As the tip of the soldier's rifle dropped, Sebastian sprang up, grabbing the butt of the gun. He shoved it up as it went off, blasting the far wall of the elevator with gunfire.

Sebastian twisted, and the gun left the man's hands. He slammed the butt into the soldier's face, eliciting a scream, and turned to help Val.

Val was an excellent soldier to have on most away missions. She was smart, and her exceptional instincts and quick thinking had saved his ass on more than one occasion. However, she was a five-foot-seven human woman, and he didn't like her odds in a hand-to-hand matchup with a young professional soldier.

Worse, he couldn't see her or the soldier who had moved on her. Her cloaker concealed both of them, but he would still try to help her. Scanning the hall, he dove in the most likely direction. A body flashed into view an instant before he slammed into it. Fortunately, it was the soldier. His wild leap pinned the man to the floor.

"Took you long enough." Val clambered to her knees and relieved the soldier of his weapons. "What the fuck is happening?" she growled as Sebastian slammed the butt of his rifle into the soldier's head. All the tension went out of the man's body.

"They have some kind of anti-magic material," Sebastian scooped a piece of glittering confetti off the floor. "That stuff Ellis was talking about. It doesn't work on our tech."

"It worked fine on Zelda," Val countered.

"Captain. You there?" Jerel's voice came over Sebastian's earpiece. They'd brought the young medic so someone experienced could administer the cure.

"I'm here," Sebastian replied

"I'm down the hall," Jerel reported.

"Move in. We're on our way."

The enemy commander had watched his soldiers disappear into nothingness and called in backup. Boots thundered in the distance as more soldiers came to join their leader. Sebastian's unit fought poorly in close quarters, and this dead-end hall spelled disaster.

"Come on!" he shouted, pulling Val down the corridor. The boots were coming from the right fork, so he went left, hoping Jerel had been smart enough to do the same.

"Mission support. I need you on that map Dr. Burton gave us," Sebastian barked. His earpiece crackled, but no one responded. Shit. Someone had jammed them.

"No wonder there was no chatter in the basement," Sebastian mused. "They've got something blocking the basement. At least our internal comm works."

In a moment, they met up with Jerel. "I watched them drag Zelda away. She was in bad shape. What the hell is that stuff?"

Sebastian frowned. "Ellis called it 'lightsilk.' She said it worked on shadow magic, but I don't think that's right. From what I can tell, it works on shadow *mages.*"

Jerel told them the soldiers had dragged Zelda into a

room at the end of the hall, and Sebastian ran over his tactical options. Decision time. They now had a rescue mission layered on the medical delivery. "You two deliver the cure to Connor and the others," he finally said. "I can't go in there anyway because of the quarantine. I'll get Zelda."

"What if Connor and the others were moved?" Val asked. It was possible, but Sebastian bet that an invading military force would have left a quarantine wing in place. *Or burned it to the ground.* Well, they would cross that bridge when they came to it.

"If they're gone, make your way back to me," Sebastian ordered. "Let's go."

Val and Jerel moved toward the medical center, and Sebastian went down the hall to where the soldiers were holding Zelda. One guard was stationed outside. He was well-armored, with that familiar fabric stretched over his gear. Sebastian looked closely at the man's gloved hands. All that covered them was a thin layer of fabric.

That was his best chance. Slinging the rifle he'd taken from the soldier in the elevator on his shoulder, he reached for his sidearm. After checking to make sure it was loaded with sleeper darts, he crept forward, aiming for the guard's hands. When he was ten feet away, he fired.

The dart shot out with a hiss, striking the guard between the knuckles. The man jumped, then looked at the synthetic blue fletching on the dart.

"What the—"

He slid to the floor before he finished the sentence. Sebastian was about to roll him aside when he had a better idea. Grabbing the back of the soldier's chest armor with one hand, he raised the limp body like a human scarecrow. As he opened the door, he flicked off his cloaker.

"You're not supposed to—" Inside the room, a young female soldier guiltily looked up from a sandwich. Her helmet rested on the ground beside her. It took her a moment to understand that something was wrong with her colleague. By the time she realized her squad mate's body was limp, Sebastian had delivered a dart into her neck.

Zelda was in the corner, her bound wrists wrapped around her knees. Her wrists and ankles had been secured with zip-ties, and it only took Sebastian a minute to cut them with his bowie knife.

"Are you okay?" he asked.

"I can't feel my shadow magic," she replied. "It burns."

He cursed under his breath. "You've gotta push through it. You'll be okay."

Her face was pale, and when he tossed the restraints aside, he saw that Zelda's wrists and ankles had small white blisters where the plastic had touched her skin. It must have been treated with the same anti-magic substance as the lightsilk.

Zelda's skin, which had been a rubbery yellow a moment before, regained some of its color as he helped her to her feet.

There was noise in the corridor, and Sebastian pulled Zelda to the wall while flicking his cloaker back on.

"Whatever's in those handcuffs, it doesn't affect our tech," he whispered.

The door opened with a shout, and a voice outside screamed a warning that the prisoner had escaped. Sebastian and Zelda remained still as the door banged closed and whoever had yelled ran off.

When they peered outside, no one was in the hall.

"Where are we going?" Zelda asked.

"Infirmary," he replied. In a remote, confused voice, Zelda protested that she didn't need a doctor. He merely pulled her along.

As they walked down the corridor, they occasionally had to push aside strands of lightsilk dangling from the ceiling. Sebastian protected Zelda as much as he could, and his cloaker held out.

He peered through the clear plastic shield on the door. Someone was moving inside the infirmary.

Ellis had told him that her father's illness was contagious for drow. She hadn't been affected, but she had encouraged him to keep his distance anyway. She wasn't sure how their different physiologies would respond. Sebastian might not have shadow magic, but that didn't make him less drow. It was possible that the virus could sicken him. Or Zelda, for that matter, and she didn't look like she could take much more.

He turned on his hush puppy and rapped a code that Val would recognize as a signal on the window. A moment later, he sighed in relief when he saw her short red hair. She poked her head out the door.

"How's it going?" Sebastian asked.

"We took out their guards." Val nodded at the corner of the room. "And Jerel is treating the patients as we speak."

"Did they put up a fight?" Sebastian asked, looking at three unconscious guards on the floor.

"Who? The guards? Or your uncle?"

"Either."

Her face darkened. "The guards went down easy. They were not prepared for our cloakers. Connor and the others were in no shape to raise objections. I'm not sure they can travel."

"Shit. We can't just leave them here," Sebastian mused.

Val looked uncertain. "The soldiers we fought were medical personnel, and the sick drow were being treated. I don't think they want 'em dead."

As she said this, someone emerged from a door at the back of the room. Sebastian nearly jumped out of his skin at the sight of the skeletal lilac-skinned figure.

Val spun. "You're not supposed to be out of bed."

Sebastian vaguely recognized Connor from Ellis' description, but she had described a man full of vitality. The drow in the doorway was stick-thin, skin sallow in his many bony hollows.

"We can't stay here," Connor ground out.

"I'm not sure you can travel," Sebastian countered. "Not if we have to fight our way out."

"Here's the thing…" Val began. His adrenaline spiked when he recognized the look on her face—a trickster's twinkle she got when she'd taken action in line with the mission that Sebastian wouldn't necessarily approve of. "What did you do?"

"We took a hostage."

Sebastian frowned. "It won't help. These are Special Forces. They'd rather sacrifice a soldier than negotiate with the enemy."

Val scratched her chin. "Well, lucky for you, I didn't take a *man* hostage. Jer, show him."

There was a long pause. Then Jerel popped into being at the edge of the room. His hands secured a tall woman wearing a navy blue skirt-suit. Dramatic white sections streaked her dark hair. She was familiar.

"Meet Senator Arden Chan," Connor announced.

Chan looked Sebastian over, eyeing the makeup on his cheeks with a searching intensity. He felt transparent, as if she could magically see his lack of a plan. The *Violet Eel* tried to keep its hands clean, and taking a United States senator hostage was *very* dirty.

Sebastian looked through the door into the hall. More soldiers were advancing, although they stopped halfway down.

"They don't want to come into the medical center. They think there is a deadly virus in here," Val explained.

"There *is*," Connor muttered before chugging Gatorade. A drow woman appeared in the doorway beside him.

"We don't need to fight our way out. We just need time."

"There's an exit at the back of the DRI. Bricked over now, but…"

"I'm sure we can find a way through," Sebastian asserted. If Zelda was still incapacitated, they would find a big hammer.

"That's what I thought," Connor agreed. "There used to be an armory over there. I have an idea."

Senator Chan's hands were cuffed and attached to a mop handle they'd jerry-rigged to keep her from running. She glared at them as she stepped outside the door.

"I'm here to relay messages," she announced in a clear voice. "There's an armory at the back of the DRI. You will clear a passage to that part of the building."

Sebastian kept his gun trained on her. "Good, Senator. That's good."

"The armory's gone," one of the soldiers shouted back.

"Tell them I think they're lying. Clear the passage," Connor instructed.

"They're not lying," Chan reported in a low voice.

Val jostled the mop handle, painfully twisting the senator's wrists behind her. "No one asked for your opinion."

"Fine." Chan took a deep breath. "*Clear the passage!*"

Several minutes later, they moved down the hall with Senator Chan marching before them as a deterrent. Sebastian leaned toward Val. "I'll stall them. You get the tunnel open."

She nodded and handed the mop handle to Jerel.

Sebastian was ashamed to admit that he was enjoying himself. The showman in him was tempted to ask for ludicrous concessions like having a jump jet delivered to the top of the Bromeliad.

He kept his requests small: pizza and a first aid kit. The first aid kit appeared almost immediately. Sebastian claimed he needed to consult his team, and he, Jerel, and Chan moved back into the depths of the DRI. There, they found a passage into the tunnels waiting for them. They cuffed Chan to a door handle.

"Who are you?" she asked as they slipped away. Sebastian didn't answer.

After they were in the tunnel, it was slow going. He, Jerel, and Val helped the others as best they could. Connor and Ilva were tired, and Ulivi was so ill that she could barely walk. In the end, Sebastian constructed a makeshift sling, and he and Zelda carried the young drow woman between them.

Connor asked questions about the cloakers, which Sebastian dodged, although the curiosity was a good sign. Maybe it was just him, but the three drow seemed to be improving already. A series of tunnels led them to a short ladder topped by a manhole cover.

Sebastian went up first and found that the ladder let out into an alley. "It's secure," he reported.

He tried his comm again. "Hello? Mission support?"

"Seb!" Ollie sounded relieved. "I mean, *Captain*. When we lost comms, we feared the worst."

"I hope you didn't send a second team in."

"No. We thought about it, though."

"Well, it's good you didn't. I'm going to drop the coordinates for pickup. The four of us are mostly fine, but send any available medical personnel."

"Copy that, Captain."

He didn't relax until they were in the van on the way back to the dock.

CHAPTER TWELVE

Unfortunately, Ellis didn't have to wait long before Lola made her next move. During that time, she went numb and slept for long, dreamless stretches. She spent half a futile hour searching for a way to write her future brainwashed self a message, but there was nothing in the room to serve her purpose. She tried scratching a message into the wall with a fingernail, but the granite was impervious.

This was it, then. When they wiped her memory, she wouldn't remember her relationship with Charlie. She supposed she wouldn't feel sad. It was such a galling injustice that she decided she should be sad now. She tried staying awake and crying, but the horrible numbness returned, the emptiness absorbing her tears before they reached her cheeks.

She guessed she was being fed twice a day, and it was three more meals before Lola appeared at her door again. Her eyes were bright, and Ellis noticed that she'd had the elder's robe hemmed. She looked more comfortable with the metal staff too, although it took Ellis a moment to realize why.

"You had it shortened," she blurted. The ancient metal rod had been clipped to a more manageable height. Pathetic. Her words seemed to destabilize Lola, and the end of her staff slipped on the rock.

"I am the elder speaker. I need regalia appropriate to my station," Lola stated primly.

"It's a shame the fancy togs didn't come with empathy or common sense," Ellis hissed.

"How droll." Lola nodded stiffly. "Get your barbs in while you remember them. In a few hours, you'll hardly remember me. I think I *will* make it a point to befriend you. Imagine that, Ellis—a future friendship, and you'll never know I ruined your life. You won't even remember your life was ruined. It's touching, really. I think you'll thank me in the end."

"Don't you dare," Ellis warned.

"I am the elder speaker!"

"If you repeat it enough times, you might actually believe it."

Lola snapped her fingers, and two tall drow men appeared at her back—younger rangers whose loyalty Lola must have won. They were also heavily armed. As they crossed the threshold of her cell, Lola turned. "If you so much as open your mouth in these corridors, I will dissolve your vocal cords and your neck with them if I have to. You will not poison the Homestead with more of your foul lies."

Ellis glanced back. The stony-faced drow guarding her looked ready to carry out Lola's orders.

Lola wanted a spectacle, so she marched Ellis through the most populated parts of the Homestead in the full perp walk. Although Ellis made no effort to escape, the guards occasionally shoved her roughly. They wanted to give Lola a show. As Ellis walked out, the whispered words "Rollo" and "Murder" floated out of the crowds of drow who had gathered to see her. Their eyes contained a mix of anger and pity.

As they wound past the last stretch of drow housing, there was a commotion ahead. The guards at Ellis' back raised their bows, and she flinched at the sound of the rawhide strings being pulled taut.

A man stood in the middle of the corridor. He was leaning hard on a cane, his body an eroded curve.

It was Sam, Rollo's brother. When he saw them come around the corner, he attempted to straighten up, but it sent him into a coughing fit.

"Stop!" he demanded, still doubled over.

The guards stopped moving. Lola glanced over her shoulder in annoyance. Apparently, she'd been willing to charge ahead without acknowledging Sam's presence.

"Stand aside," Lola ordered. The faces of the drow lining the corridor wrinkled in dismay at her tone.

"No. This is wrong," Sam protested.

"I know it seems like a memory wipe is letting her off easy, but it's best for everyone," Lola countered.

Sam looked disgusted. "I'm not worried about letting Ellis off easy since she didn't do anything. She was in the room with Rollo, so she couldn't have shot him."

Lola's fists clenched into vibrating balls. "She led the conspiracy."

Sam snorted. "Who shot that arrow?"

Lola was taking deep breaths, unsuccessfully trying to contain her anger. The surrounding drow looked skeptical.

"You don't know, do you? If Ellis *did* lead a conspiracy, wiping her memory is the worst thing you could do. How are you ever going to find her collaborators?"

Lola's voice was thin and tight, stretched to its breaking point. "Ellis was debriefed. You'll see progress on the investigation soon."

"Ellis Burton didn't kill my brother!" Sam shouted. Raising his voice so it carried through the passageway strained his lungs, and his words gurgled at the end as a spasm set him to coughing again. Lola froze until he spoke again. "My brother trusted Ellis."

"A mistake that cost him his life," Lola snapped.

"No, I don't think so. Ellis would never have hurt him. Neither would Trissa or Landon. You're killing an innocent woman," he wheezed, doubled over, his torso resting on his cane.

"I'm not killing anyone," Lola shot back.

Sam shook his head, then barely managed to raise it. "All we are is our memories. Something's wrong." He looked around. "You can't let this happen. The path will lead us into the burning light."

The drow guards tensed, facing the crowd. The Homestead was wary, but they weren't compelled to act. Not for her.

"Stand aside," Lola ordered.

"No." Sam's voice was quiet but firm. "Stop this madness and release Trissa."

The chatter from the crowd sharpened when he

mentioned the healer. Ellis might not be the most popular girl in the cave, but Trissa was beloved.

"Trissa has not been detained. She's working on a special project," Lola corrected.

"Then how come she hasn't visited me in weeks?" Sam demanded.

"Perhaps she lost interest," Lola spat. The crowd hissed. They were turning against her, and she knew it. "I don't have time for this," Lola announced. "We have an appointment in the speaking chamber."

Ellis locked eyes with Sam, sending him a silent message of thanks. It was a relief to know that one person would remember the truth. When her memory was gone, he could tell her what had really happened.

As they pushed through the crowd that had collected around Sam, Ellis' back was tense. She thought the crowd might turn violent and a sharp elbow might attract a knife in response. Sam didn't back down, forcing Lola and one of the guards to bodily remove him from the passage. They shoved him against a wall, and he collapsed to the floor.

Lola was showing the Homestead who she was.

After that, they detoured away from the populated sections. Lola seemed disgruntled. She had clearly envisioned a triumphal march with a chastened Ellis jeered by throngs of drow. Instead, there was thick tension and unease. Upset by the tepid response, Lola picked up the pace, moving swiftly down the gentle slope that would bring them to the speaking chamber.

"You've finally returned to the scene of the crime," Ellis muttered as two drow in uniform stepped aside to admit them to the chamber. They were young, and their uniforms didn't fit properly, a running theme with Lola's crew.

Maybe the elders could help her. They were smart, and more than that, they were wise. Ellis doubted they'd swallowed Lola's snake oil. As the guards pushed her down the spiraling walkway at the edge of the chamber and she saw the elder council, or rather, the former elder council, her hope guttered.

Katya was pale and drawn, looking out-of-place in white crystal silk trousers and a tunic. The old drow looked little better than Ellis. As she drew closer, Ellis realized that only five of the six people in the knot were elders.

The sixth was Trissa. Ellis let out a cry of excitement, and Trissa winced. Her eyes slid away from Ellis toward several makeshift wooden tables of equipment. These contained a variety of dried mushrooms, potion bottles, and sharp-looking knives.

The wooden tables were arrayed around a granite slab resting on two boulders. Eight feet long by six feet wide, the top was etched with shadow magic symbols. Ellis wondered where the elders kept the monstrous thing. It was old and worn in places. One of the elders was carefully re-carving runes on an eroded section.

"What is that?" Ellis asked, voice quavering.

"It's for the spell." Lola's eyes gleamed.

When they reached the bottom, Lola strode over to Katya. "Is it ready?"

"Almost," Katya replied dully. "These things can't be rushed."

Lola's expression soured in disagreement. "This is just a test run. It won't count until you treat Irving."

"You are asking us to use our most powerful magic. You might take that lightly, but we do not."

"Why are you doing this?" Ellis asked, turning to Katya with a pleading look. To her surprise, the old drow looked sympathetic.

"Lola detained my grandchild in the tunnels," Katya explained. "She has full control of the rangers as well."

"She has my son," Donnel reported.

"Where's Nell?" Ellis asked, looking for the sixth elder.

"She was a disagreeable old hag with no family." Katya sounded half-affectionate.

Lola growled. "She understood the consequences when she decided to oppose me. Unless you want to join her, I suggest you make a different choice. Trissa is an acceptable substitute for Nell. Assuming that she wants to keep Landon alive."

Trissa looked at her feet.

None of these people had willingly helped Lola. "We are as free in our choices as you," Katya stated softly, putting a hand on Ellis' wrist.

Ellis had wondered how Lola had taken control of the Homestead so quickly, and now she knew—brute force and coercion.

"It's not too late to stop." Ellis turned to Lola. "The drow won't stand for this forever. They already see through you, and eventually, they'll stop you."

Lola didn't answer. She just slapped her face. Ellis was so numb that it barely hurt. "Get on the table," Lola ordered.

Ellis didn't think she could get away. Any of the elders could stop her with shadow magic, although considering the circumstances, Ellis doubted that they would leap to Lola's defense. She wouldn't just lie down and let them erase part of her, though.

"If you let me go, I'll confess publicly," Ellis offered. "I'll never tell anyone what happened here. Just let me keep my memories."

Lola paused in the middle of inspecting a row of polished crystals on a small table by the slab.

"If I want your confession, I'll write it myself and forge your signature." She waved a hand and turned away. As Lola's long white waves swung toward her, Ellis made her move. Digging her feet into the stone, she grabbed an arrow from the nearest guard's quiver and lunged toward Lola's back, bringing her fist down in a furious arc.

The hit didn't land. The nearest guard pulled Ellis away before she could bury the arrow in Lola's back. When Lola accepted the arrow from the guard, she feigned nonchalance, but the small hairs on the back of her neck were standing up.

"Are you *sure* we can't knock her out?" Lola asked.

"No. She has to be conscious," Katya explained.

"I won't cooperate," Ellis snarled.

"Suit yourself," Lola replied with a wave. "If you want them to do delicate neuro-magical work while you thrash about, that's your prerogative."

"I don't recommend it," Katya countered. "What we're doing is...new territory for most of us. We bear you no ill will, but we are bound to see it through." She broke eye contact and turned to Lola. "The preparations will take some time."

Ellis slid onto the table. The stone was cold and hard

beneath her. A few times, she met Trissa's eyes. The healer's movements were as graceful and efficient as always, but there was something out-of-place about her expression, as if she were struggling to hold in a secret.

Ellis looked away and forced herself to think about Charlie. If this was her last chance to remember him, she would take it. Her mind ranged over the details of their first date—or first murder investigation, depending on how you looked at it. His lips had been warm during their first kiss. Each memory was a stab in the guts.

Her blood had healed him. The idea that part of her had been with him at the end was morbidly comforting.

Finally, the preparations were done. Ellis would die, and a new Ellis would be reborn. Hopefully, an Ellis that resembled her in some way, but who knew? Maybe they would screw it up, and she'd be a vegetable.

The elders began placing crystals on her body, and she forced herself to breathe slowly. The rhythm became second nature as the crystals vibrated with the Earth at a languid but steady frequency. The rocks pulled her down, welcoming her.

The table rattled beneath her. Tranced out, Ellis felt it remotely. Perhaps it was part of the spell. The table rattled again, and grit hit her in the face. Ellis' eyes flew open.

The ceiling was falling. Far above, the rock was moving, shaking pebbles and sand loose. Maybe it was a metaphorical image. Ellis' mind was collapsing, and it was creating this image as a way to process the experience.

Gravel hit her in the collarbone. "*Ow!*"

"*Stop that!*" Lola screamed.

"We're not doing anything," Katya protested.

Ellis blinked as more gravel hit her cheek.

A hole was opening in the ceiling. It started small, barely long enough to insert a pen in, then widened. Strong hands grasped Ellis and yanked her off the table as a chunk of rock the size of her fist hit the spot she'd been in. Katya looked at Ellis, panting, her marine-blue face tight with effort. More rocks fell, and Katya's fingers slipped away from Ellis' clothes.

Shit.

As Lola and her guards fled the rockfall, Ellis rolled under the stone slab. There was a crash as more stones fell, and something heavy landed on the slab above her head.

Ellis looked up as one of the guards at the edge of the room raised his bow and aimed an arrow at her head.

No, not her head. The guard was aiming at whatever had landed on the table. Ellis' eyes widened as the taut bowstring snapped in two, the loose ends whipping the guard's face. He howled in pain.

There was another *thud* on the slab, and then the rocks stopped falling. Lola, who had been cowering behind one of her guards, surged forward, shadow magic balling in her hands. The air temperature dropped, and there was an odd noise like a hydraulic puff of air. A silver net flew forward and wrapped around Lola's body. The air temperature returned to normal, and Lola's screams turned desperate. *"Kill them!"*

More guards ran in, but before they could leap down a single terrace, an invisible attacker clothes-lined them. Ellis rolled out from under the slab. On top of it, a familiar figure peered down at her. It took a moment for the lilac features to register.

"Dad!" Ellis cried. *"Ilva!"*

Connor Burton leapt gracefully down from the slab as his partner loosed an arrow at Lola. The arrow dissolved just before it hit Lola's torso. "Are you okay?" her father asked.

"I think so. They were going to wipe my memory."

She wondered if she had forgotten anything. She didn't think so, but there was no time to work that out now.

Connor pulled Ellis to her feet. "We have to go."

"Don't move," Lola shot back.

Ellis looked up and cursed. Ten feet away, Lola had her arm around Trissa's throat. A very sharp ceremonial knife was in her hand, and the blade quivered against Trissa's pale skin.

Connor's fingers flexed, then stilled. He couldn't dissolve Lola's knife in time, and not without taking out a chunk of Trissa's throat.

"Put your weapons down." Lola backed up the spiral walkway with her hostage in her grip.

Ellis dropped her fists to her side, and her father dispelled the shadow magic in his hands. As she wound her way up with Trissa in her grip, Ellis thought about what they could do, but there was nothing.

When Lola reached the rim, she shoved Trissa through the entrance. Ellis and Connor sprinted toward her, but it was too late. Raising both arms above her head, Lola cast a shadow magic spell on the rock ceiling, and a chunk the size of an elephant fell, blocking the entrance.

"She cast a ruin-web!" Connor shouted. "The whole thing will fall in a minute. We have to go!"

The hole in the ceiling was a discouraging two stories

above them. Ellis couldn't jump that high, but before she could look for other options, there was a flicker of movement above her, and a rope snaked out of the dark center of the hole. It fell in loops, the end dangling just above the slab. Connor threw her onto it, and Ellis got her bearings, then shinnied up.

As Ellis ascended, she realized she was still half-dazed. The steady movement of the rope sliding in her palms would have sent her back into a trance if falling rocks hadn't constantly jolted her back to reality. When Ellis reached the top, Sebastian peered down, gripped her hand, and pulled her up into a narrow passage.

"Run!" he shouted, shoving her. The tunnel wasn't tall enough to stand up, and Ellis scraped her head on the ceiling as she sprinted, half-hunched, up the slope. She heard footsteps behind her, but they were drowned out by falling rocks. Ellis looked over her shoulder and heard Sebastian scream as his foot slid into a widening crack.

"*Keep going!*" he shouted.

Ellis ignored him and retraced her steps. The rock under their feet shivered again, and Sebastian screamed at the crack's vise-like pressure. Katya and Donnel were behind him, blocking the view of the tunnel. Had her dad made it up?

"*Hold still,*" Ellis shouted. She put one hand on each side of the crack and took a deep breath. As her adrenaline surged, she pushed with every ounce of strength in her body.

The rock cracked, and Sebastian hauled his foot out. "Holy shit!" he said, staring in amazement.

"*Come on!*" Ellis cried, pulling him along.

Sebastian grunted when he put his weight on his foot, but he kept moving. Ellis, turning back to keep an eye on him, realized that Katya and Donnel had their eyes closed. Their hands were stretched toward the rock, brushing it on both sides.

They were counteracting the ruin-web, an impressive feat for people fleeing in terror. As Ellis ran down the passage, the shaking subsided. She nearly cried in relief when the tunnel let out into a cavern. One by one, their group spilled into the space, straightening as they left the passage.

Ellis held her breath until her father came through the narrow entrance. She restrained the instinct to fling herself into his arms. He was still unwell and underweight, although his skin had returned to a saturated lilac, much better than it had looked for months.

"You're okay!" she exclaimed.

"The medicine worked very quickly. It was like magic."

"Claire would blow a gasket if she heard you say that." Ellis smiled.

"A silver lining," Connor replied mildly.

Coming up beside Connor, Ilva frowned at the mention of Ellis' mother.

"How did you get in without anyone noticing?" Ellis asked.

Connor cleared his throat. "When you were a child, your grandmother and I built several tunnels in remote parts of the Homestead. I thought it was...possible I might someday need to remove you swiftly."

"From, say, an angry mob?" Ellis asked.

Connor nodded. Ellis sighed. "Apparently, that was a reasonable fear."

Sebastian joined their circle. "He's told me a lot about Elandra. I'm even sorrier that I never met her."

Now that they were standing next to each other, Ellis realized that Sebastian resembled her father. Sebastian's face was still smeared with makeup, but some of it had sweated off, and his lilac freckles were the same color as Connor's skin.

"We should only rest for a moment. We must leave the Homestead before Lola and her band of traitors realize we escaped."

Ellis accepted a bottle of water from Sebastian. Draining half of it revitalized her, and after she wiped her mouth, she cleared her throat. "No."

Connor frowned. Ilva looked vaguely impressed.

"We're not going to flee. I agreed to help Sebastian with…a project."

"He told us about the ring," Connor assured her.

"Val's going to kill me, but if I can't trust Nan Elandra's boy, who *can* I trust?" Sebastian asked.

"I have to get my shadow magic powers back. Trissa was working on it, and she kept good records. Maybe she solved it."

"You want to steal her notes?" Connor asked.

Ellis nodded. "I can't ask you to go with me." She said it automatically, then realized how ridiculous that sounded. She didn't have her shadow magic back, so she would not be able to sneak through the Homestead to Trissa's lab on her own. "Scratch that." She sighed. "I need your help."

"Yes," Connor agreed. "We'll get those notes."

CHAPTER THIRTEEN

Percy laid his hand on the large German Shepherd. The dog tensed, hackles rising. Percy petted him slowly and deliberately.

"You're okay," he soothed.

"Ivan's not a people person." The dog's handler, a thin man named Gus, unconsciously leaned away from the pair.

"Hullo, Ivan. He's all right," Percy stated.

The dog's consciousness was a nervous squiggle, all uneven edges. When his hackles went back down, Percy gently reached out. *Hi.*

Mind spiking at this psychic intrusion, the dog growled, ears back.

"That's why we call him Ivan the Terrible," Gus explained.

You're not terrible. You're adjusting. This is all new, Percy thought. *And very strange.*

The dog's growl became a low woof. Percy stroked his fur again.

"Can I take him into the other room?" Gus asked, tugging on the leash.

"We've barely gotten past small talk," Percy grumbled.

Micah, the guard at the door, regarded them with extreme skepticism. "Come on, man. I joined the military to get away from woo-woo shit."

Percy was keeping mental tabs on Ivan's psychic state, but he replied, "Now, now. The United States military has a long history of paranormal investigations. The CIA once tried to assassinate Fidel Castro with mind waves."

"They shoulda learned from their failure," Micah shot back.

Do you think we can be friends, Ivan?

The dog's tail twitched. Not a wag, but a positive sign.

What's your favorite treat, Ivan? Percy asked.

An image of a small pillow-shaped dog treat appeared in his mind. Ivan's tail wagged as he remembered biting into the cheesy interior.

"Can you get me some of his favorite treats?" Percy asked. "Size of a thumb and filled with cheese?"

Gus looked uneasily at Micah. "How did you know that?" the handler asked, hand twitching on Ivan's lead.

"Woo-woo shit," Percy said drily.

This might be a terrible mistake. He didn't like having agreed to be Arden Chan's personal lab rat, but he also couldn't let Rose and the others be transferred to a CIA black site. At least he was making new friends. Gus reached into his pocket and pulled out a bag of the treats that Percy had described, which were smaller than what Ivan had shown him. Apparently, the treats loomed large in the dog's mind.

Percy plucked one from the bag and held it out in a flat palm. Ivan snuffled it down, tail a metronome.

"He's supposed to do a task before you reward him," Gus grumbled.

Percy glared. "I'm not *training* Ivan." He was unable to keep the annoyance out of his voice. "I'm *befriending* him."

"What's the difference?" Gus asked.

Percy shook his head. Some people were hopeless.

I'm sorry to rope you into this so soon, but I was wondering if you might do me a favor. My friends are in trouble, and I'm trying to help them.

Ivan plopped onto his haunches and cocked his head. The dog didn't have many friends besides Gus, an unreliable treat dispenser. The dog's mind went jagged at the edges, then calmed.

Help. Help, yes. Friiiiieeeeeendddd. Help a friend.

Ivan's tongue flopped out. When Percy scratched him behind the ears, the dog licked his hand. *I need you to tell me what you see in the other room. That's all. A little information.*

See. See. See friend, Ivan responded.

Percy nodded at Gus. "Okay, go ahead. See you later, Ivan."

Gus twitched the leash and led the high-strung German Shepherd away.

"You need to let that dog chill out once in a while," Percy offered. "Play fetch. Run around."

Micah stared after Ivan's retreating hindquarters. "Huh."

Percy took several deep breaths to ground himself. Then he sent his consciousness after the dog and his handler, bumping into the minds of the people in the room. These were usually too complicated for him to get much insight into.

Ivan? Are you there, friend?

The dog went crazy, his riotous barking audible through the thick concrete wall. *Friend? Friend? Can't see friend. Smell friend a little.*

That's right. I'm still in the other room. Maybe I need to shower. Percy tried to keep his thoughts genial, but a lot was riding on this, and he fidgeted in the plastic chair. A bit of his anxiety made it into his conversation with the dog, and there was another round of barking.

Smell! Smell friend! Faraway and close!

I know it's weird, buddy. You'll get used to it. I really need your help. What do you see?

There was a long pause, then a cluster of mental static that Percy struggled to decipher. Dogs didn't communicate like humans. It took trial and error to be understood.

The barking stopped. *Tree.* The dog said. *No smell tree, but tree.*

A brownish triangle flashed into Percy's mind. *Look at it for longer.*

The brownish triangle resolved into a classic pine tree, only it was too perfect, and the needles glinted weirdly. Percy squinted.

Ball! Ball! Ball! Ivan began barking again. That was clear. This time, the frazzled energy of the dog's mind was joyful.

"Come on back in," Percy shouted.

"Drop it!" Gus barked. A moment later, nails clicked on the concrete as Gus led the dog back into the room.

"Do you have to touch him again?" Gus asked.

Percy shook his head. "Not unless he wants more petting."

Ivan strained toward Percy, and Gus let the leash out. The dog trotted over, and Percy scratched his chin. *Thank you very much, Ivan.* He suffused the thoughts with warmth, promising future treats. Ivan's tail wagged.

"Well?" Gus.

"There's a Christmas tree in there. Artificial, if I'm not mistaken. Glittery."

From the way Gus' eyes widened, Percy knew he'd hit the target.

"You told him." Gus poked a finger into Michah's chest.

"Not me, man. I haven't even been in there. Those were the rules."

Ivan barked, offended. *Me! Me! Me! I tell friend!*

"There was also a ball," Percy added.

"Oh, yeah? What color?" Gus demanded.

"Not sure. Dogs only see blue and yellow. Whatever it is, Ivan's a big fan. Aren't you, boy?" Percy found the dog's favorite spot just behind his right ear.

"Fuck," Gus snarled.

"What? It's good, right? This is what we were looking for," Micah replied. He was tracking Percy more closely now, his gaze nervous. The hair on the back of Micah's arms stood straight up. Percy should be used to it, but the fear in Micah's eyes stung. It was easier when people didn't believe him.

Percy crossed his arms. "I held up my end of the deal. Now you hold up yours."

Ivan tentatively licked his knee. *Ivan bad? Bad dog? Make friend sad.*

Percy tried to smile, but it was no use. The dog knew. *No, Ivan. You're a great dog. I'm just really gonna miss my friends.*

During his next meeting with Senator Chan, she seemed disgruntled. She was wearing a turtleneck under her blazer, and when she scratched the skin, he thought he saw a bruise. And she seemed jumpier than normal. It made Percy wonder, but he didn't pry.

Chan reported that Rose, Charlie, and Mikhail had been debriefed and released. She thanked him for his honesty and recited cliches about service to his country. She even brought him some terrific vegan Pad Thai.

In the following weeks, Percy dearly missed his previous boredom. His days became a tangle of tests and demonstrations. First, he had to repeat his trick with Ivan in front of Gus' boss, the leader of the Army's K9 division. That guy had to loop in *his* boss. Each new person seemed to believe that their underlings had been conned, but each time, Percy convinced them.

Finally, a four-star general arrived, a reserved man with salt-and-pepper hair and a uniform crisp enough to shut a drill sergeant up. There was a small plastic case under his arm that turned out to contain a ferret.

"Hello, son," the general greeted, although they were almost the same age. "I'm General Marlon Jarwell, and this is Wiffleball." He tapped the plastic case, and a pointy black-masked face appeared by the wires.

Percy sat up straighter, suddenly interested. General Jarwell was the first military officer who had bothered to introduce the animal he'd brought with him. The military was mixing things up. Percy sighed. "What do you want me to do this time?" he asked as the general gently placed the cage on the table. "Send a message? Identify a playing card?"

"I'd like you to ask Wiffleball what's wrong," the general replied. The corner of his mouth twitched. Was the man embarrassed?

Percy narrowed his eyes. "I don't understand."

"You don't have to prove anything to me," the general told him. "You convinced my best people that you're the real deal, and they've never given me a reason to second-guess them. I would like you to ask my daughter's ferret what's wrong. He's a year old, and he isn't thriving."

Percy's eyes opened. This was a pleasant surprise.

"Wiffleball, you said?"

The general coughed. His aide, standing at attention at the door, was holding in a laugh at great personal expense. When Percy looked closer and saw the ferret's thin frame and patchy fur, he didn't think things were very funny.

Hello, Wiffleball, Percy began. A wan squeak emerged from behind the bars. *I'm Percy. It's nice to meet you.*

The ferret's energy was a drab gray ball. It moved closer to the bars.

"You've taken him to a vet?" Percy asked.

"We did. It wasn't very helpful."

Percy popped open the cage door. The ferret mustered the energy to walk onto the table, staring curiously at Percy. It sniffed the surrounding air.

Room. Big room. The ferret assessed the interrogation room, seeming a little more lively.

"Why don't you leave Wiffleball here overnight?" Percy

suggested. "We'll get to know one another, and I can tease out what's going on."

The general looked dubious. "All right, but know that I will make a bad enemy. My daughter is very attached to her pet."

"I'd rather swallow my tongue than harm an animal." Percy stared at the man.

"I believe you," the general replied. "I'm not sure what we're going to do with you."

"Other than analyze the brass' pets?"

"Yes."

They were both quiet. After a minute, the general nodded and strode out.

"That thing looks like a worm that got stuck in a cotton candy machine," the guard at the door offered, watching the ferret make a slow circuit of the table.

He doesn't mean that, Percy told Wiffleball. The ferret squeaked softly.

"I'm tired," Percy stated. "I'd like to go back to my cell."

"You have another doctor's appointment this afternoon," the guard reminded him.

Percy winced. He'd been poked and prodded plenty since he'd demonstrated his powers. They were going to do brain scans, and he didn't relish the thought of being cooped up in a big tube for hours.

The guard saw his expression. "Since the general's given you a new mission, maybe we can push it back."

Percy smiled.

As it turned out, Wiffleball was very observant and a pretty good conversationalist as far as ferrets went. Percy was glad for the company, but he also had ulterior motives.

He wanted to understand the layout of the prison. Since coming here, he had only seen a single hall, which had his cell on one side, the interrogation room on the other, and the medical center at the end. To have any hope of escaping, he needed to know more.

Hope might not be wise, but he had it. Only way to live, in the end. So, as he lay on his cot, playing fetch-the-kibble with Wiffleball, their conversations got more directed.

At first, he'd been concerned that Wiffleball might be too ill to help, but as they conversed, a picture emerged: the general's daughter, who appeared in Wiffleball's mind as a skyscraper-tall blonde demon, was subjecting the ferret to a wide range of cosmetic treatments. She had tried to dye his fur blue with a kit she'd purchased at CVS, which had caused hair loss she'd attempted to treat with increasingly fragrant body lotions. There had also been lipstick and eyeshadow incidents.

Percy wasn't going to tell the general that, though. Not for a few days, at least. No need to rush through this friendship. It was also possible that the man wouldn't believe him. Sometimes, even very intelligent people were blind when they looked at their children.

Wiffleball, I was wondering if you could do me a favor.

Sleepy. The ferret spent a great deal of time as a furry donut on the end of Percy's bed.

After a nap?

A hesitant squeak. Percy explained what he wanted and left it up to Wiffleball. There would be more animals in the future if this didn't work out. That was the only way they'd be able to keep testing him. The ferret was wary but settled into a nap and let out a low snore. When he woke up, he ran up Percy's chest for a scratch behind the ears.

Ready. Ready.

All right, Percy thought. *I'd like you to explore this floor. See if you can get past any of the doors.*

The ferret squeaked affirmatively. Percy went to the door and listened for the sound of footsteps. Then he opened the slot through which the guards slid his meals. It was just tall enough for Wiffleball to squeeze through. Getting back in might be a problem, but Percy would worry about that later.

Wiffleball slid down the door onto the tile floor, then found his footing. Percy let him go where he wanted to. It would be more fun for the ferret that way. Fortunately, the ferret went down the hall to where it met a corridor running to the left and the right.

Like to run run run. No space in cage at home.

You can run all you want with me, buddy. Percy would add "more room to roam" when he debriefed the general. When the ferret reached the end of the corridor and peered to the left, an image of two looming shapes appeared in his mind. Soldiers.

Try to stay out of sight, Percy suggested.

The ferret pulled back. A moment later, the soldiers passed. A patrol, maybe? Wiffleball followed them.

Wiffleball gave an excited mental exclamation. *Ferret door!*

Percy wondered what the hell a ferret door was. Wiffleball sent him a mental image, and he realized it must be another cell with the same food slot that Percy had sent Wiffleball through.

See if you can climb it.

Wiffleball ran to the door and placed his paws on the smooth surface. He scrabbled there for a minute, but the door was too smooth, and the food slot was too high.

Maybe not ferret door. Wiffleball thought.

That's all right, friend.

Something happened to startle the ferret, sending its mind into a tangled flurry.

Show me what's happening, Whiff.

The ferret sent Percy an image.

The food slot had opened, and a face was peering out. Percy recognized the chipped pink nail polish and red hair. It was Rose.

His fury sent Wiffleball spinning. *Bad. Bad? Bad!*

No. Sorry, bud. You're doing great. Good ferret. Great ferret, even.

Senator Chan had lied to him. Rose was still here. A military prison bunker was better than a CIA black site, but only by a hair.

That's my friend Rose, Percy thought. *She's great. The best.*

Rose's face disappeared from the slot. Percy was disappointed, but she reappeared a moment later, dangling a strip of blanket through the food slot and down to the ferret. Wiffleball gratefully ascended.

Smart woman. Percy rushed over to shred his blanket. Rose had solved the problem of how to get Wiffleball in and out of their cells.

Same. Same-same-same. The images Wiffleball sent Percy gave him déjà vu. Rose's cell was identical to his. She was standing with her arms crossed. Even in her gray military sweatpants, she looked beautiful. Less glamourous, but fiercer. After peering at the ferret for a full minute, she raised her hands above her head and clapped three times.

What? What-what-what?

Wiffleball had not been inducted into Percy's animal network and didn't recognize the signal, but Percy did.

Go say hello.

Wiffleball shot forward, circling Rose's ankles in a dramatic figure eight. She sat down on her cot, and the ferret ran up her leg. She eyed the ferret's disheveled fur uneasily for a moment, then reached out and petted him with gentle fingers. Wiffleball squeaked happily. *Smells good. Lady smells good. Not like monster.*

Percy guessed that "Monster" was what the ferret called his preteen tormentor. He was suddenly jealous of the ferret.

After a moment, Rose pulled a pen and a yellow legal pad off her bed. Percy wondered how she'd finagled that. Maybe she'd offered to write a confession. As Wiffleball perched on her shoulder, she scribbled something on a small scrap of paper. Rolling it up, she unraveled a string from the raw edge of her blanket and secured the scrap. Then she looked at Wiffleball.

The ferret didn't understand what she was saying. Animals rarely did, or not at first, anyway. If they talked to Percy long enough, they started to pick up language. Sometimes, he felt uneasy about that. Who was he to dictate what went on in an animal's mind? He could worry about that later. He understood what Rose wanted.

Can you bring the paper back to me? he asked, supplying helpful images. The ferret squeaked warily but allowed Rose to tie the scrap to his neck. Scratching his head, she carried him to the food slot, lowering the strip of blanket again so the ferret could climb down instead of sliding.

Can you come back to me, buddy? You can go for another walk later.

The ferret's mind went red with frustration, but then it cleared, and he made his way back to Percy's cell. This time, no one was in the hall, and soon, Percy was re-admitting the ferret to his cell, scrambling to gently retrieve Rose's note.

Guards are liars, the note said. Then, *Miss you* at the bottom, along with a big heart. Percy brought the note to his nose, half-expecting perfume. It only smelled like paper and ink, and he felt stupid. The military didn't issue prisoners Chanel No. 5.

Although he wished for her sake that she was far away, the thought of Rose being so close was comforting. "Excellent work, Wiffleball," he whispered. "Great ferreting." Wiffleball squeaked, and Percy lay back, planning his next move.

CHAPTER FOURTEEN

They left the elders behind in the chamber when they went to look for Trissa's notes. The five drow were shaken, but they had lived too long to quickly admit defeat. The last time Ellis looked over her shoulder, they were cross-legged on the floor in a tight knot, their heads together. They had not cast a muffling spell but were speaking too quietly for her to hear them from a distance.

Ellis did not mistake their calmness for ambivalence. Katya nurtured a fury perceptible in her eyes. Rather than act rashly, however, she was channeling the red-hot emotion into planning, supported by her peers.

As they reached the hidden entrance to the Homestead, Sebastian pulled Ellis into a private conference.

"Here." He handed her a small device and explained how it worked. The cloaker produced an eight-foot invisibility sphere around its origin point. When Ellis' hand wrapped around it, she felt a surge of shame. She should be able to turn invisible without mechanical assistance, and the device felt like a mockery.

"What's wrong?" Sebastian asked.

"It feels like...cheating. It's not real shadow magic."

Sebastian's lip twitched, but he hid his annoyance. She hadn't meant it as an insult, but he had taken it that way. *He'd* never had access to shadow magic. "It'll *really* make you invisible."

"Sorry." Ellis gestured apologetically. "I didn't mean—"

Sebastian waved the apology away. "The cloakers can't be dispelled by lightsilk. How's *that* for real?"

Ellis' curiosity spiked, and she spent a minute discussing what Sebastian had gone through at the DRI. Taking it in was a struggle. "We never should have trusted Chan."

Connor, who had joined them, shrugged. "I never did."

"We can debrief more after we get out of here," Sebastian suggested.

"You're right," Ellis agreed. "Let's focus on the potion."

She flicked the cloaker on. Techno-invisibility would take some getting used to. She could feel the change in air temperature but not the shadow magic. Normally, she could adjust the invisibility envelope on the fly, extending or retracting it depending on the circumstances. With the cloaker, she was stuck with eight feet. Anyone who got closer would see her.

"Skilled shadow mages can sense it," Sebastian added. "So try not to wallop them with the envelope."

"Copy that." Ellis passed through the gap in the rock wall into the Homestead.

Trissa's laboratory shared a wall with the infirmary. Unfortunately, the fight in the speaker's chamber had caused more than a few injuries, and the corridors were packed with drow carrying messages, delivering supplies, and checking on loved ones. They had to double back through the halls several times before they could slip inside Trissa's lab. Lola had not reassigned the space, and it looked like Ellis remembered. The desk was piled with scrolls and journals, which Ellis divided into two stacks, sliding half to her father. Sebastian paced just inside the door, peering into the corridor to watch for interruptions.

Most of the written material on Trissa's desk was patient records. There was an extensive journal detailing Sam's medical history, including a range of treatments Trissa had attempted. Ellis carefully set it aside.

Three-quarters of the way through the remaining stack, she found a scroll of potion recipes. There were at least fifty variations of the formula, with notes on what had worked and what hadn't. Ellis thought about the potion that had turned her purple. She'd been so excited about it that she'd made Trissa record the recipe. Scanning the list, Ellis' blood rushed to her face when she realized the ingredients on the scroll matched her memory.

"This is it!" Ellis tapped a formula in the middle of the scroll. Connor peered over her shoulder.

"But I don't recognize some of these symbols." Ellis hoped Trissa hadn't written the recipe in an indecipherable code.

"It's alchemists' annotations," Connor murmured, pulling the document out of her hand.

"You can read it?"

"I taught her." He unrolled the scroll to the end. A quarter of it was blank, so he read the last recipe on the list. "This one has no brewing notes. She must have been working on the recipe when Lola launched her coup. I don't think she ever made it. Or tested it, obviously."

"Can *you* make it?" Ellis asked. "Do you think it will work?"

The tip of Connor's tongue stuck out as he focused on the document.

"I might make a few adjustments," he murmured. "But yes, I can make it." He glanced at the walls in the lab. Small batches of mushrooms grew from every surface, a crazy quilt of glowing caps. Connor scribbled a list on a piece of paper. "We need these."

Ellis nodded and got to work picking mushrooms. She didn't pick too many in case they needed to make another batch. Their first stumbling block came halfway down the list. "We need purple pinheads. There aren't any in here."

Connor sighed. "There's a patch in the mushroom caverns."

"All right," Ellis said. "I'll go."

"No," Connor said. "You're too visible. I can move undetected, and even if someone sees me, I might be able to talk my way out of it. I haven't lost *all* my clout in this place, no matter what Lola has done."

"All right."

Connor waited for an excruciating few minutes until the chaos in the hall died down. Then, moving quietly, he twitched his fingers and popped out of existence. A second later, the curtain opened and closed.

Sebastian stretched out on a cot at the edge of the room, looking relaxed.

"Seeing you and Dad next to each other, you look a lot alike," Ellis mused. "You've got regal noses."

Sebastian touched his nose self-consciously, but she thought the comment pleased him.

"I'm glad he'll be okay for your sake, but for mine too. I never knew Elandra, and after Mom died, I didn't think I'd get any more relatives. It's like having a tiny piece of her back."

"Thanks for coming to get me," Ellis murmured.

"You're our King Arthur," Sebastian stated with a grin. "We can't just leave the sword in the stone."

"Still. I appreciate it."

"Well, you're welcome. I wish we'd been able to come through the front door. Usually, we don't contact drow communities in mid-coup."

"It worries me how quickly Lola and her cohort took over," Ellis grumbled.

Sebastian didn't share her anxiety. "You shook things up with the Outpost. When you open peoples' minds to change, things don't always change for the better."

Ellis bristled. "Are you saying that Lola and those other assholes are *my* fault?"

"This isn't about blame," Sebastian shot back. "I'm just saying that the *Eel* has been doing this kind of thing for years. We should have brought you into the fold earlier. Taught you our ways."

He was too exhausted to varnish his opinions, and Ellis bridled at his dismissive tone. "I don't need anyone to teach me. I've been doing just fine."

"Oh, really? Opening your Homestead to a coup is 'just fine.'"

Ellis' anger came out like a geyser. *"At least I'm a shadow mage."* It's not true, idiot. Not anymore.

Worse, the insult slid off Sebastian's back. "You think me having to use a cloaker somehow makes me *less?*" Sebastian asked. Ellis, who realized this was the worst insult that had come to mind, was ashamed by how little the barb had affected him. "Not only does the cloaker make me just as invisible, but we discovered that it's immune to lightsilk. Arguably, it makes me *more* powerful."

"It's not affected by lightsilk?"

When Sebastian explained the events at the Bromeliad, the implications were interesting. And it made sense. Lightsilk worked via skin contact with a drow shadow mage. The cloakers were mechanical, their shadow magic concealed. They sat in tense silence for a few minutes.

Sebastian had come to rescue her, and he was family. Straightening, she offered, "I'm sorry. It's not your fault that you don't have shadow magic."

His lip curled. Her apology had annoyed him, and she spent a second wondering why.

"You think of my lack of magic as a tragedy I'm not responsible for, but it's not. It's just the way I am. *You* think that the things that make you different from the other drow..." he gestured to indicate the walls and the wider Homestead beyond, "are flaws. You think the way you look is a flaw. You're never going to be able to develop your gifts to their fullest if you think they're only good for compensating for your human heritage."

Ellis was furious since he was right. Being half-human weighed down one end of the scale, and she'd always envisioned her magical abilities as balancing it out. Considering their current mission, he was hypocritical to criticize.

"You *need* me to be a shadow mage," Ellis pointed out. "I can't use the ring with a cloaker, can I?" She would think about using her shadow magic to compensate later. Her father had never insulted her appearance, but he *had* urged her to use shadow magic around other drow and had seemed proud when she performed a difficult spell.

He had also pushed her to complete the tunnel rites the instant she was ready, insisting that it would make her part of the drow community. Had she not been part of it before? Would he have felt the same about her if she wasn't a shadow mage?

"What are the other drow communities like?" Ellis finally asked. There was a community in Montana south of Glacier National Park on the border with Canada. She had never gone there, although when she was in her teens, one of the drow in her creche year had visited his family and brought back stories.

"It varies quite a bit." Sebastian told her about several of the communities he knew of. Lots in Iceland and Scandinavia, where there was overlap with folklore about the fey. She noticed that he was cagey about actual locations and details. If you worked in clandestine ops long enough, the clandestine part apparently became second nature.

Forty-five minutes later, Sebastian told Ellis a story about two drow communities who had merged and started a new homestead after clashing with humans too many times. Rebuilding the homestead must have been exhausting, but the prospect of creating a new society thrilled Ellis. Ellis would make lots of changes to the Swallow's Nest if she rebuilt it from the ground down.

She was about to ask a question when a low rumble of

voices rose in the hallway. Ellis sprang up and went to the curtain across the door, wondering if her father was back. Instead, she heard running footsteps and shouting.

Something serious was happening, and a crowd was moving toward the speaker's chamber. In their wake, the curtain slid aside, and an invisible person barreled into Ellis. Connor popped into sight a moment later.

"What's happening?" she asked. As she spoke, a second person appeared behind her father. Ellis blinked in surprise. It was Landon.

"*Ellis!*" her brother shouted.

"*Lan!*" Ellis threw her arms around him.

"I...took a detour." Connor clapped his son on the back.

"That wasn't the plan," Sebastian barely looked at Landon.

"Plans change," Connor stated. There was a moment of tension, but Sebastian didn't seem inclined to spoil the family reunion. "The drow are rising up against Lola and her band. We ran across the elders in the eastern spoke, marshaling a group of loyalist rangers. Landon's guards weren't eager to sacrifice themselves to the cause. But they *will* notice that he's gone, so we have to get out of here."

"Do you have enough time to make Trissa's potion?" Ellis asked desperately.

"Nice to see you too, sis." Landon smirked. "Glad you have your priorities in order."

The sarcastic quip was so *Landon* that Ellis threw her arms around him again, and he squirmed. "It *is* nice to see you," she agreed. *He sounds like his old self.*

"Okay, okay!" Landon weaseled out of her hug.

Connor smiled at his children's reunion. "We don't have

time to make the potion here. For all we know, Lola might try to cave in the Homestead if she thinks she will lose this battle."

"She wouldn't do that," Ellis protested. "Would she?"

Connor sighed. "Some people would rather burn the world down than admit defeat."

"We have great science facilities on the ship," Sebastian offered. "Assuming we can get there. Plenty of equipment for working with mushrooms, too."

"We'll find a way." Ellis was halfway to the pile of mushrooms on the desk. Moving quickly, she loaded them into cloth bags.

"We have to help Trissa," Landon stated desperately. "Lola is still holding her hostage."

Connor's reply was low, urgent, and discouraging. "We can't. Lola might not have a knife to her throat, but she's being held in extremely close quarters. Any move we make would put her in more danger."

"I don't want to leave without her," Landon countered.

Ellis thought about the ring and the power that it promised. "We'll go after her. But right now, we have to leave. Lola won't hurt Trissa. She needs her as a hostage so she has leverage on us."

"I hate the thought of leaving without her," Landon growled.

"So do I, but we don't have a choice." Ellis squared her body, resolve hardening. "Move, people! We don't have a lot of time."

A moment later, they were standing at the door, laden with potion ingredients.

"We should go out through the Trunks," Ellis suggested.

"The tunnel network there is relatively open, and if they block one exit, we can find another."

Connor nodded, his mouth a thin line.

Sebastian tossed her a cloaker. "Thank you," she said, guilty about her earlier insults.

They moved down the hall in a tight formation. The drow they passed hardly looked up, hurrying from place to place with their eyes on their feet. The recent changes in leadership had exhausted them and weighed them down.

Twice, groups of Lola's lackeys rushed through a cross-tunnel in the distance, but Ellis and her band avoided collisions. When she pulled Sebastian up the final rungs of the ladder and onto the forest floor, Ellis was exhausted. Unfortunately, they were still miles away from help. "Tell me you have a helicopter."

He sighed. "It's on my Amazon wish list."

CHAPTER FIFTEEN

Percy sat in his chair, stroking the silky back of one of the many Army canines his captors brought in to work with him. This was an alert Doberman pinscher. Percy sent it calming thoughts and tried to keep his voice soft. "You can bring me all the dogs you want. I'm not doing anything until I talk to Arden Chan."

"That's not part of the program," Sergeant Henderson said. He was the younger of the two soldiers, the newest addition to the research project.

"I'm not sure you understand the situation," Percy countered. "I was cooperating before. I'm not cooperating now. I might cooperate again, but first, I need to talk to Senator Chan."

The two soldiers conferred briefly in the other room. When they returned, their faces were stony. "Our orders have not changed, Mr. Rawlings."

"I think you'll find they have."

Wiffleball had left that morning. Percy was sad to see the indomitable ferret go, but he'd had a stern conversation with General Jarwell about not letting his daughter use makeup and perfume on her pets. Jarwell had sighed. "I guess you can't put lipstick on a ferret any more than a pig."

"You can, but you shouldn't," Percy told him. "Some things are just wrong." He'd said that pointedly, although he wasn't sure Jarwell picked up on the subtext.

When Percy made it clear that he would not be participating in the day's research and that no amount of drill-sergeant-flavored yelling would change his mind, his guards returned him to his cell. They took his books and paper, too. All he had to entertain himself with was his anger at their betrayal.

Rose was still down here, so Charlie and Mikhail were too. He was less concerned about the young Russian's well-being, but badly behaved puppies sometimes became good dogs, so perhaps the young man would learn.

Over the course of the next day, soldiers with increasing numbers of bars on their shoulders and fancy gold bits on their lapels visited him. Some brought carrots and some brought sticks, but he refused to budge.

There was a risk that they would physically harm him. The United States government wasn't above torture. So far, no one had threatened him with that. *Maybe they don't want to break their fancy new toy.*

Whatever their motivations, they eventually met his demands. When they finally led him into a room containing the senator, she was angry. "I had to cancel lunch with my top donor, so this better be good." She still seemed jumpy. Percy wondered again if something had happened to her over the past few weeks.

"You lied to me," Percy began gruffly, slumping in his chair. On most of her visits, Chan brought Percy coffee or a snack. Today, she pointedly slurped a blended iced coffee without offering him one.

"Can you be more clear?" Chan asked.

"Rose and the others," Percy said. "Charlie and Mikhail."

Chan waved her hand, frowning. "You and I made an agreement. We let them go."

Percy frowned. "You did not. Rose is down the hallway."

"Someone's given you misinformation." Chan scoffed. "I'll have a word with the soldiers."

"If you take two left turns from my cell, you'll find her," Percy corrected. "Long red hair. Hard to miss."

Chan blinked. "You don't have access to that part of the facility." She looked at the soldiers for confirmation.

"Let's just say I weaseled the information out of someone," Percy shot back.

It took her a moment to figure it out. "That fucking ferret." She gritted her teeth.

"Nice guy. Very curious about his surroundings."

Posture changing, Chan laid her hands on the table and looked into Charlie's eyes. "The United States government doesn't negotiate with terrorists. You broke into a top-secret weapons facility, an act for which you show no remorse. You are going to remain in government custody for the rest of your natural life, as are your companions.

"The deal has changed. You are going to participate in research into your unique psychological abilities. You are *also* going to tell us everything you know about the attack on the institute, the Outpost, and the individuals you call the drow. The more you tell us, the more pleasant your captivity will be. I can make your life very difficult. I can make Rose's life very difficult as well."

Percy winced. Chan saw it and smiled, smelling weakness. "I know you two are close," the senator purred. "Play your cards right, and I might allow a visit."

Percy's mind raced. Cooperation was no longer an option. He could not assume that anything these people told him was true. As remote as the possibility of escape was, he had to pursue it. An idea blossomed in his mind, and he forced himself to look meek. It wasn't a stretch. He'd never been an intimidating guy.

"You could do that?" he asked, trying to make his eyes pleading. The A/C was on full blast, and he only had to hold them open for a minute before a tear welled in the corner. *Ooh, that's good.*

"I can do whatever I want. Your privileges are contingent on your continued participation in the research and your general willingness to talk."

Percy nodded slowly, pretending to think. Charlie still had his new shadow magic powers. It was possible—likely, even—that the guards didn't know about them. "There is one thing..."

Chan leaned closer.

"This isn't exactly *intelligence*," Percy started, "But it might help you get more info. It's a little tidbit about Charlie."

Chan leaned even closer. "Oh?" Her face was pleasant again, and she slid her half-finished coffee toward him. Percy took a long sip, then thanked her and leaned back. "Charlie's afraid of the dark. Phobic, actually."

Chan's face fell. It wasn't the coordinates for a secret

underground drow lair, but she clearly wanted to encourage openness.

"That *is* an interesting tidbit," Chan agreed soothingly. "Thank you very much, Percy. I'm sure we'll talk again soon, and I look forward to seeing results coming out of your research project."

"Can't wait," Percy replied, twisting the tie on his sweatpants between two fingers.

Percy wasn't a violent man. He had been a lifelong vegan, although he occasionally bought meat for the animals in his care. He didn't blame carnivores for their natures, but there were certain people he would try to save from a room with a hungry lion in it. Senator Arden Chan was no longer one of them.

Want bite? Bite lady? Percy heard the question from the Doberman pinscher in the hall as Chan walked past.

No, thanks, Percy replied. Tempting, but he didn't want to get the dog in trouble. *I'll get my revenge soon.*

CHAPTER SIXTEEN

Ellis tilted the glass, watching the swirling purple trails run down the sides. It looked like all the others, and she tried to contain her expectations. Sebastian had cleared the lab, although Val had stayed. Ellis wasn't thrilled about the first officer's irritated presence, but she didn't complain. Landon and her father had stayed to support her.

"I modified Trissa's formula slightly," Connor explained. "Based on my experience. I thought I could get a little more out of a few of the trumpet varietals."

Ellis sniffed the tumbler. Earthy and mineral notes hit her nose. "Did you see Mom?" she asked.

Connor nodded reluctantly. "She checked on us. Ilva and Ulivi and me. She was smug about how well her cure worked. Now, are you going to drink your potion or continue to play with it? We went to a great deal of trouble to make it for you."

There was no sense in putting it off longer. Ellis took a deep breath, brought the glass to her lips, and took a healthy sip. The earthy liquid tasted familiar on her tongue, although she noted the modifications. Her anxiety spiked as she swallowed. Then a mellow coolness spread from her stomach through her body.

A pool of shadows under the lab bench drew her eye. The tile floor in the darkest corner intensified, dancing with pinpricks of purple. Tendrils of power brushed her ankles.

It was back. Her magic was there, but could she use it? Ellis stretched her hands out. The last time she'd cast a shadow spell, it had been unbelievably painful. *You have to be brave.* Breathing deeply, she pulled at the darkness. When magic surged toward her, she flinched, waiting for pain or some other psychic blow, but nothing happened. She felt ordinary. Tears welled in her eyes.

Connor frowned. "Are you in pain?"

"No. I feel great." Ellis grinned. "Turn off the lights," she requested eagerly. Sebastian strode over to the nearest switch and flicked it off.

The darkness came alive, the shadows intense and immediate. Letting out a whoop, Ellis pulled the nearest globule of power into her hands. She took several deep breaths to calm herself before she got overexcited and dissolved a hole in the hull. Instead, she flattened the swirling purple tendrils into familiar sheets, then tossed them up like a skein of silk. Her skin cooled as the magic floated on top of her, turning her invisible.

When Ellis disappeared, the people in the room reacted in various ways. Sebastian let out a cheer. Connor merely smiled.

"Would you let our research team study that potion?" Sebastian immediately asked.

Connor stiffened at the word "research."

Ellis twitched her fingers to dissolve the invisibility bubble. "Not right now, Sebastian."

"Can't keep the Skip's mind off work," Val opined cheerfully from his side.

"Speaking of which..." Sebastian tossed the ring box across the bench.

Ellis caught it in one hand. "We should wait another minute to make sure there aren't side effects."

"Spoilsport," Sebastian shot back.

Truthfully, Ellis was just as eager to see what would happen. She liked the *Violet Eel* and its crew, and she was excited about gaining an important place among them. So far, her shadow magic wasn't exploding or causing her pain. Toying with her restored abilities, Ellis cast a muffling spell and another invisibility spell, then pulled an empty cup out of the trash and dissolved a smiley face in the side. When she finished, she was beaming.

Sebastian had been right. She shouldn't have *needed* shadow magic to fit in with the drow. But he had also been wrong. It wasn't meaningless. The dark power entangled in her fingers was no small thing. She loved working with shadow magic. Wrapping up her spell spree with a final dismissal, Ellis opened the ring box.

She wasn't prepared for the blast of magic that hit her in the face. Ellis had only seen the ring through the *Violet Eel*'s special goggles, which allowed non-magical people to see powerful shadow magic objects. With her magic restored, the ring was ablaze with power. It flowed toward her, exploding from its confinement in the ring box.

Ellis looked closer. A dark, dense corona of magic

encircled the ring. Now and then, tendrils arced away like plasma loops on the surface of the sun. It was beautiful.

And she was going to wear it.

Greedily plucking the ring from the box, Ellis slipped the metal around her right pointer finger.

Nothing happened. Ellis stretched out her hand, and the black pearl danced in the shadows.

"Well?" Sebastian asked, sounding disappointed.

Wait. Just wait. Bone-deep anticipation gripped Ellis, and when she waved her hand, the pearl darkened. Not the color, or not exactly. There was a change in intensity and a shift in the fabric of reality. The pearl seemed to vanish, replaced by an identically sized hole, black and light-sucking.

Ellis brought the ring to her face to inspect the edges of the hole. The surrounding air and light fell into it like sand running through an hourglass. Ellis knew she should be afraid. Any reasonable person would be alarmed by a hole in the fabric of space, especially one that was getting bigger. She should rip the ring off her finger right now, tie it to a cement block, and drop it into the ocean.

She didn't. She watched in amazement as the hole ate the surrounding air until it was as big as a quarter, then big enough to stick her hand through. Ellis plunged her fingers through, expecting silky darkness.

Ellis gasped when she realized what the hole contained. It was shadow magic so thick it was hard to move.

Imagine what I could do with all that power.

The hole was still growing. It was now the size of a basketball hoop, and the viscous magic inside gently tugged on her arm, pulling her close. She hardly needed to be pulled. Ellis was desperate to know what was inside this rip in existence. The ship's laboratory had faded and become flat, much less real than this new world.

The magic tugged again, and Ellis took a half-step forward. Her booted toe caught a rough place on the lab's floor and she stumbled, then fell into the rich fog of magic on the other side of the portal.

She fell for a long time, a slow glide through the dark magical aether. There was nothing to look at except swirling purple, but she was not bored. Her body felt alive. Her skin was responsive to the pressure of the magic around her, her eyes enticed by infinite configurations of violet and gray.

A pinprick of light appeared below her. As she floated toward it, the pinprick grew, and she saw that it was a platform, a disc floating in a dark magic sea. It was waiting for her.

Ellis landed lightly on the pale disc. The platform was larger than she'd realized—distances were difficult to judge with no external reference point. The platform was flawless and about twenty feet in diameter, although it wasn't flat. In the center was a raised circular structure. The edge of a pool, she realized, walking closer. The silver liquid was reflective, and Ellis immediately knew not to touch it. Not because it was dangerous but because it would be wrong to disturb the perfect mirror smoothness.

Ellis stared at her pale face, framed by dark hair and dense shadows. Something moved in the reflection, and Ellis spun. There was nothing behind her, but the reflection had changed. When an image began to form in the pool, Ellis understood that the silver surface was showing her something. Her face remained in focus, but the background changed, the shadows rearranging themselves into loose shapes.

The shapes were fuzzy at first, the edges blending with the world around them. After a moment, they resolved into a clear picture. It was a cavern; Ellis knew that much. A drow cavern, she guessed, from the mushrooms glowing on the walls. Not any species she recognized, but her gut still said, "Drow."

In the center of the cavern was a statue hewn from the same abyssal marble as the walls and floor. A hooded human of medium height and build. Their outstretched hand held a sword. The hilt was forged from familiar-looking black metal—the substance the ring was made of.

The blade was something entirely different. *It's made of darkness* was Ellis' first thought, but it missed the mark. The blade wasn't made of darkness. The blade was made of *nothing,* of absence. A curved scimitar of negative space culminating in a point so sharp that the edge disappeared. What would you cut with a blade like that?

Ellis guessed the answer was "Anything."

Her reflection blinked. Ellis was surprised—a trick of the light?—but then mirror-Ellis smiled and held her finger to her lips. Ellis watched as her reflection spun, raven hair billowing behind her.

So that's what the back of my head looks like.

Ellis' reflection strode to the statue and wrapped her hand around the hilt of the sword. With a mighty tug, she pulled it free. Ellis-in-the-mirror raised the blade triumphantly, and as she did, the ring on her finger let out a purple sunburst that screamed shadow magic. The magic circled the impossibly black non-blade until it shone.

Ellis' reflection walked back to her. She felt uneasy as her mirror-self approached, as if this sword-wielding version of herself might try to escape and replace her. Her reflection lowered the sword as the cavern disappeared.

"Do you understand?" her reflection asked. Ellis realized that she, too, had spoken.

"Understand what?" she asked desperately. Her reflection mouthed the words as she spoke.

"The ring is the key. Find the lock."

The surface of the pool rippled as Ellis' reflection reached up her silver hands, grabbed her head, and pulled her in.

This time, her fall was neither long nor gentle. She was only in the silver liquid for a moment before the world shifted and brightened, and she plummeted toward the rough, familiar floor of the *Violet Eel*'s laboratory. Her ankle twisted under her as she landed, and she tipped sideways into a gray metal lab stool. Strong hands righted her before she turned the room into a game of science dominoes.

The light overhead was too intense, so Ellis shielded her eyes with one hand as she tried to get her bearings. Deep inside, an invisible cord pulled at her, a distinct directional tug on her skeleton, originating in her left pointer finger. The black metal ring was ice-cold, and when Ellis touched it with one finger, the pull got stronger.

That-way-that-way-that-way, it repeated insistently, and Ellis took two steps toward a poster on the wall outlining how to use the laboratory's eyewash station. Was the ring trying to send a message?

Do I have something in my eye?

No, the ring's insistent message was not about the wall or even the boat. It was telling her where the sword was, or the general direction. She inhaled sharply at the revelation. The ring would happily pull her off the side of the boat as long as she kept moving in the direction it wanted her to go. She struggled to remain still.

The faces of the people around her, drow and human, were drawn and worried. When Sebastian rushed in to help her to her feet, his eyes were bright. "What happened?" he asked excitedly, pulling her closer to the light. He stared eagerly at the ring, not meeting Ellis' eyes.

"You disappeared," Connor reported, looking concerned.

"Do you mean I turned invisible?" Ellis asked. The vision had felt so real.

"I don't think you turned invisible. I think you were gone," Connor mused.

"I watched through the shadowglasses," Val chimed in from the edge of the room, tapping a pair of goggles that glowed faintly purple. "And I didn't see an envelope of magic. I didn't see anything."

"Where did you go? Do you know how to wield the ring now?" Sebastian asked.

"Sort of." Ellis pulled herself onto a stool and removed the band. The tug disappeared. She retrieved the ring box, but she couldn't let go of the ring, not now. Tugging the string out of her hoodie, she slid the ring through it and pulled it over her head. The metal was cool against her breastbone.

Ellis explained her journey to the floating stone platform. "The ring...it-it's only part of the picture. I don't think it's what you were looking for. I think you're looking for the sword." She shivered at the memory of the dark curved blade.

"Did you bring it with you?" Sebastian asked.

"The sword? No. It wasn't in the...vision or whatever that place was. The whole thing was more like a magical video file, waiting to play for whoever put on the ring."

Sebastian considered. "A message."

"Yes. The ring isn't the artifact. It's like the keys to a car. It will activate the sword once I find it."

"You know where it is?" Sebastian asked.

"Not exactly, but I know how to find it," Ellis told him. There was a faint vibration over her heart.

Sebastian leaned forward.

"I'll tell you everything I know. But first, we have to rescue Trissa."

Val cursed and kicked the lab bench. Sebastian's face turned red around his deepening purple freckles, and he glared at Ellis, restraining himself before his anger exploded. "I know you miss your friend, but that's not the priority right now."

"Like hell, it's not!" Landon shouted, squaring up with the captain. "You don't know anything about *our* priorities."

"You owe her," Ellis insisted. "She invented the potion, and without it, I wouldn't have been able to use the ring."

"I'm not ungrateful," Sebastian stated formally. "But this

isn't about you or me. It's about the plans my crew has been working on for years."

"With all due respect, I'm the only one who can use the ring, so it *is* about me. I say we rescue Trissa first. Have you heard anything from the Homestead?" Connor was still in communication with several of the rangers. They occasionally texted during their surface patrols.

Connor paused. "Yes. Lola didn't have much loyalty beyond her immediate circle. There's still some fighting in the Homestead, but the elders have regained control."

"Did they capture her?" Ellis asked.

Connor shook his head. "Lola appears to have fled. She…took Trissa with her as a hostage."

Landon pounded a nearby table. "I'm going to kill that woman."

"We have to find her first." Ellis turned to Sebastian. "Can you help us?"

Val had sidled over to the captain, and the two exchanged looks born of long familiarity. "You're gonna show her the Violet Eye, aren't you?" Val asked angrily.

"What's the Violet Eye?"

Sebastian sighed, ignoring Val's fury. "Come with me." He gestured for Ellis and the others to follow.

Ellis skipped after him, her excitement rising. She sensed that he was about to hand her the missing piece of the puzzle. He didn't explain himself, however, staying silent as he led them deep into the ship's underbelly, down a narrow ladder to the level that housed the mechanical systems. Just before they reached the engine room, Sebastian stopped in an ordinary stretch of hallway.

"Did you bring us here to show off the fire alarms?" Ellis asked, glancing at the wall's only adornment.

Sebastian shook his head and reached for a line of rivets along a seam in the corridor. Ellis blinked in surprise as he pressed the rivets in a complicated sequence. There was a hiss, and the seam widened before swinging out like a door. A whir spilled out, and Sebastian ushered them into the room beyond.

It was a server farm. Ellis just gaped. The large, narrow space ran at least half the length of the boat. Blinking computer towers stood at attention on both sides, busily whirring. Large transparent tubes pumped murky seawater around the equipment. Here and there, components glowed with shadow magic. "What is this?" she asked, enjoying the chill.

"When you're building a supercomputer, one of the biggest problems is cooling," the captain told her. "My tech team could explain it better, but all those ones and zeroes turning on and off all the time create a lot of heat, and that's not good. Fortunately, we have a readily available solution." He touched the nearest tube of seawater.

"What do you do with it? Run the systems on the ship?"

Sebastian shook his head. "No. The Violet Eye is much more powerful than that. We use it to track drow activities."

He led her between the rows of servers to a workstation at the end of the room.

"I wish Percy could see this," Ellis murmured to her father.

Connor nodded in agreement.

"The hacker who believes he's a pet psychic?" Sebastian

asked. "I never understood why you got mixed up with that guy."

Ellis bristled at Sebastian's casual dismissal, but now was not the time to argue for the existence of animal psychic powers.

"How does the Violet Eye work?" she asked as he sat down at the workstation.

Sebastian typed as he spoke. "When we started, all it did was look for keywords in videos and posts, things like purple skin, invisibility, elf, or cave. It put together a big report, and we had to sort through it manually. Now, we use machine learning. The AI can sift the data on its own, although the crew still reviews it once in a while to keep the system current. And of course, we monitor communications in the communities that have adopted modern human technology, which is pretty much everyone."

"That's an invasion of privacy," Ellis stated.

Sebastian shrugged. "It's for their own good. Until now, deep intelligence was our best weapon against threats to the drow *and* human communities. It's how we stop major threats." He raised an eyebrow. "If you'd prefer, we can look for Lola the old-fashioned way. Val went through the Green Rangers' survival school, so she can try to pick up her trail in the forest."

"We'd have to send a ground unit, and it might take me a bit to get back up to speed on my tracking," Val agreed, falling easily into the role Sebastian had assigned her.

He nodded. "In an abduction case, time is the most important thing. But if that's how you want to handle it..."

"No. We can use the Violet Eye." Ellis didn't like the way he'd twisted her arm.

Sebastian typed code into a user interface. From long familiarity with Percy, Ellis was prepared to leave him be for a few hours, but when she turned to go, he caught her arm.

"Wait. We're searching in a pretty small geographical area. This won't take long." He was right. Within a minute, a running tab of information appeared on the screen, including newspaper clippings, transcripts of 911 calls, snippets of police radio conversations, Instagram posts, and photos stored in the cloud. Ellis was impressed, but she was also alarmed. This was a huge amount of information for one person to have.

Sebastian, accustomed to the readouts, scanned it. "Got her."

"Really? Already?"

"I think so. There have been a couple reports of a purple-faced woman stealing from houses in the Lake Arrowhead area. Lola easily could have gotten there from the Homestead. Val, you still around?"

"Whaddaya need, Skip?" his first mate asked, coming forward.

"We need that ground team after all. Put it together. Take Ellis. I'll assign someone on this end to feed you fresh intel as it comes up. Let's take Lola down."

After barking a quick affirmation, Val was gone like a shot. The captain touched a button on his watch and had a quick conversation with someone on the other end. "All right. Let's go."

CHAPTER SEVENTEEN

Lake Arrowhead was an hour and a half outside of the city. It was a pretty stretch of water surrounded by wealthy Angelenos' second homes. Evergreen trees grew everywhere, but the forest was illusory. "It's a suburb pretending to be woods," Val muttered as their van wound its way around the lake. There was hardly a patch of ground not visible from the window of one vacation home or another.

The *Violet Eel* stored a handful of vehicles in a public garage in Long Beach. That was easier than tricking out a rental. The interior of this panel van was old and shabby, brightened only by the expensive surveillance equipment behind the driver's seat. The away team consisted of Ellis, Val, Jerel, and Ollie.

According to the intelligence from the Violet Eye, Lola was moving in an easterly direction, breaking into houses for supplies as she went. They were heading to the first of the burgled houses in the hopes of picking up information. It was perched on a steep hill and had a balcony and a driveway that angled sharply down into a small garage.

Closer inspection was thwarted by the presence of a work truck. Three men in brown coveralls were maneuvering a large panel of glass down the steep driveway.

"I doubt Lola stuck around for window repairs. Let's keep going," Val suggested.

The next house that had reported a break-in was just down the road. Someone had tripped the security sensor, although, according to the confused conversation between the owner and security company, the burglar had not been visible on the security feeds.

"She's being reckless," Ellis commented.

"That makes her dangerous," Val replied. "It's hard to fight an enemy who has nothing to lose."

The next house was located farther from the lake at the end of a long gravel driveway. Val parked on the side of the road a few houses down, and Ellis and Val approached using cloakers. One of the windows on the large blue house was boarded over, and while they inspected it, a rent-a-cop security car idled up the driveway. The not-very-perceptive guard driving it made a bored circuit of the house. Ellis and Val easily avoided him.

"We should keep moving," Ellis told Val. They had just climbed back in the van when Val got a call from the *Eel*, telling them another break-in had been reported.

"Law enforcement?" Val asked. It wouldn't help anyone to send their strike team crashing into a bunch of local cops.

The crewmember manning the Violet Eye told Val that so far, the information hadn't traveled further than a few texts between neighbors.

"Then we'd better move fast." Val depressed the gas

pedal, and they sped around the rim of the lake, catching occasional glimpses of silver water through the trees. Val pulled the van onto the shoulder near the house and activated a large cloaker. "It won't stop someone from walking into the vehicle, but they won't be able to see it from the road."

As they crept through the forest, Val donned a pair of glowing purple goggles. "If Lola's invisible, we'll get her," Val assured Ellis. At her side, Jerel and Ollie were screwing unusual-looking sights onto thin dart guns.

"What is that?" Ellis asked, pointing at a glowing purple crystal attached to the barrel of the dart gun.

"Shadow scope," Ollie replied gruffly. "It's drawn to shadow magic. Helps a lot when the target's invisible."

"You can see invisibility spells through those goggles?" Ellis asked, shocked. A shadow mage paying attention could sense invisibility spells, but it took a lot more effort than looking through a pair of violet-tinted glasses. Sensing shadow magic took attention, concentration, and, occasionally, luck.

That train of thought reminded her to take a sip of the shadow magic potion. The dark pockets in the undergrowth at her feet immediately intensified, brushing her ankles with chilly tendrils.

"No offense, Ellis, but I don't know you, and I don't want my team tripping over you," Val offered.

Some offense taken. "No problem." Ellis slowed her stride, and Ollie and Jerel passed her.

Ellis didn't doubt her abilities on the front lines, but there were benefits to hanging back. For one, it gave her the opportunity to watch how the team from the *Violet Eel* moved. They knew each other well, and Val was a confident, capable leader. However, something about their way of working made Ellis uneasy, and it took her a few minutes to realize why.

They move like the DRI's soldiers.

The déjà vu resolved in a rush of dread. They *were* hunting a drow in human society.

Val whistled, and the team halted in formation. Peering through the violet goggles, she pointed to a hollow at the base of a fallen tree, then made a hand sign. Ellis wanted to ask what the sign meant, but a hard look from Ollie stopped her.

It became clear when two crew members surged forward. With surgical precision, Ollie unfurled a lightweight net across the hollow while Jerel aimed his gun. As soon as the hunched, no-longer-invisible figure in the hollow popped into view, Ellis rushed forward.

It was Trissa. She screamed for the men to stop, but Jerel ignored her and popped off two darts in quick succession. Trissa twitched and went still as Ellis reached Jerel, leaping in front of the gun.

"Stop! That's Trissa!"

It was too late. The young drow woman was as still as death. Ellis remembered with a start that she now had access to her healing magic and reached toward her friend with both hands, only to shy away as she realized Trissa was covered in a lightsilk net, or whatever the crewmembers of the *Violet Eel* called the fabric they used to dispel shadow magic.

"Is she dead?" Ellis demanded. She almost punched Val in the face when the older woman rolled her eyes.

"She's just knocked out," Val assured Ellis.

"Why did you shoot her?"

"Because she's an unfamiliar drow in enemy territory. My motto is, 'Knock 'em down and sort 'em out later.'" In the middle of this recitation, her head spun to track a movement in the distance.

Ellis tried to sense the presence of an enemy shadow mage but only felt the normal press of dark magic along the ground. "What is it?"

Val didn't bother to answer, just whistled sharply and ran around the side of the house. Jerel and Ollie followed. Ellis itched to join them, but she couldn't leave Trissa alone while Lola was in the area.

She searched for a stick and, working as gently as she could, used it to remove the glittering net from Trissa's body. Then she leaned down near her friend and checked her heartbeat and breathing. Both were steady, and Ellis decided she shouldn't use healing magic without knowing what Trissa had been injected with.

The crashing noises in the forest disappeared with a pop. *Hush puppies.* Ellis waited tensely, extending her shadow magic out in searching ripples. *I should have asked for a pair of those special goggles.* She was using a lot of shadow power trying to sense magic the old-fashioned way, but her potion bottle was mostly full. She took several more sips as she waited. The sky was overcast and gray, broken up by thick banks of clouds. As one of these moved across the hazy sun, the shadows at Ellis' back shifted, and she sensed something.

The hitch caught her attention. Turning, she focused her magic in the direction of the disturbance, sending out fine, sensitive tendrils. They bumped into the disturbance in the area of a large, flat rock. Exactly the kind of rock Ellis would have chosen to stand on if she hadn't wanted someone to see her footprints in the grass.

If she hadn't been so focused on the rock, she would have missed the sound of a bowstring being drawn taut. Instinct sent her diving into a nearby bush as an arrow hit the ground where she'd just been. It lodged in the dirt a hand's breadth from Trissa.

Ellis disentangled herself from the shrub, twigs and leaves digging into her skin. Another arrow whistled toward her, but the dense vegetation slowed it to a crawl, and it merely grazed her skin.

She instinctively reached for her shadow magic, and for the first time in a long time, it was there. She pulled big ropes of it into an invisibility shield, although she was rustling the vegetation around her so much that it would not disguise her location. Still, any advantage was worthwhile. Ellis dodged two more arrows as she zigzagged into the dense forest, then took a chance and swung up on the low branch of a pine tree. She crouched and watched the ground for signs of movement. The invisible attacker was Lola. It had to be.

Twigs crunched from the direction of the house, and Ellis guessed that Val's party was returning. She peered through pine needles as the three *Violet Eel* crewmembers popped back into existence. Jerel and Ollie were carrying an unconscious man.

It was Irving. Ellis' heart sank. Of course Lola had brought her brother with her. She hoped living under open skies had helped Irving with the claustrophobia he'd developed during his DRI captivity.

"Watch out!" Ellis screamed at Val as an arrow lodged in Jerel's shoulder. It should have hit his heart, but Lola had aimed wide to avoid hitting her brother. Looking down from her branch, Ellis saw something glittering on the ground. The branch with the lightsilk net. Was there a way to use it?

Val's team had abandoned Irving on the forest floor and taken cover behind a stand of pine trees. *Where is Lola?*

Ten feet away, a depression appeared in a small patch of grass—a footprint. Lola was moving toward her brother. It was now or never. Planting her boot against the trunk at her back, Ellis pushed off and sailed toward Lola's location.

Her arms windmilled, but she'd aimed well, so she slammed into Lola where she'd expected. The young drow dropped her shadow spell in surprise and struggled as Ellis pinned her to the ground, her violet skin beaded with sweat. Lola went limp, and Ellis relaxed, but it was a ruse.

Lola tensed, grabbed a stray arrow from the dirt, and made a wild swing, but it was a weak attack, and Ellis easily batted it away. After punching Lola in the stomach, Ellis scrambled for the lightsilk-wrapped stick. She found it and swung it toward Lola, pinning her to the ground. It didn't seem to hurt her, but Ellis sensed Lola's shadow magic draining.

"I've got eyes on the target!" Ollie shouted nearby.

"Ellis, get back!" Val screamed. Her tone was so intense that Ellis jumped away, leaving Lola in a pathetic tangle. The crew of the *Violet Eel* had turned off their hush puppies. Ellis was still getting her bearings when Val pulled a marble-sized object off her bandolier, pressed two buttons, and chucked it toward Lola, who had flung the lightsilk net aside and was pawing through the grass for her lost bow. There were two beeps before the marble exploded into a dense purple six-foot sphere.

Dissolution magic.

"No!" Ellis screamed, but it was too late. The purple sphere dissipated, leaving a perfect bowl-shaped depression in the ground.

Everything inside it was gone, including Lola. The only thing the grenade had missed was a trailing hank of lilac hair.

Sebastian Altamont had built a dissolution magic grenade.

"All clear!" Val shouted. She displayed no emotion, just scanned the forest for more shadow magic. Ellis dropped her invisibility spell and ran toward the shorter woman, fists raised.

"Why did you do that?" She took a wild swing at Val.

Val caught her fist and gave Ellis a warning look. Ellis was a lot stronger, and they both knew it, but there was a question in the first officer's eyes. Did Ellis *really* want to test her? Would Ollie or Jerel hesitate to use shadow magic grenades if she attacked?

Ollie had crouched by Jerel and was administering first aid. To Ellis' relief, Jerel was correcting Ollie's form with the sharp eye of an experienced battle medic.

"You murdered her." Her disgust welled when Val rolled her eyes.

"She was dangerous, and she was shooting to kill."

"I had the situation under control!" Ellis shouted. "You didn't have to kill her."

Mistakes happened in the heat of battle, but this hadn't been a mistake. Worse, Val seemed unaffected by the fact she'd just killed someone. Ellis remembered what Sebastian had told her about Val's loyalties. You were either in or out with her, and if you were out, she would happily kill you without losing sleep. It turned Ellis' stomach.

Jerel was still conscious but getting paler by the second. He needed the kind of medical care you couldn't administer on a camping trip.

"Will he make it to the *Eel*?" Val asked Ollie.

Ollie was about to say something when Jerel raised his head. "In my professional opinion, yes," he wheezed.

When Ollie nodded in agreement, Val said, "Load him in the van. Ellis and I will take care of the detainees."

"Trissa's not a detainee," Ellis stated. "And Irving...he's sick. He deserves help, not jail." The only person who'd been able to keep him calm was his sister, and now she was gone. Dissolved out of existence.

"They're detainees until I say otherwise," Val corrected. "Now, do you want to get in the van, or do you want to stay here and wait for cops to show up?"

Instead of answering, Ellis went to Trissa and bundled the young woman into her arms for the walk back to the road.

As they wound away from Lake Arrowhead toward the dock, Ellis wondered if she was in or out with Val. She was in no rush to find out.

CHAPTER EIGHTEEN

That night, Ellis' exhaustion didn't bring her anywhere near sleep. The battle in the forest hadn't been the last of their ordeal. Irving had woken up in the van in a panic, and Val had almost driven off the road as Ollie had struggled to contain the drow while trying to inject him with sedatives. Trissa, who was half Irving's size, was still asleep when they loaded her onto the ship.

Ellis had tried to see her, but the doctor had turned her away. "She's dehydrated and hasn't eaten for a few days. She's in no shape for visitors."

In the middle of the night, after an hour of staring at the ceiling from the eerie quiet of a hush puppy bubble, she went to find her father. He and Ilva had been given cots in a corner of the *Violet Eel*'s storage bay.

They weren't sleeping, either. They were sitting on the floor on makeshift chairs they'd crafted from supply boxes, playing a board game. She almost laughed when she saw the box.

"Candyland?" Ellis asked.

"We're exploring human culture," Connor explained.

"If this is human culture, humans are dimwitted sugar fiends." Ilva flicked the plastic arrow on the game's spinner.

Ellis lowered herself onto the floor beside them and toyed with a deck of cheerful pink cards.

"Is something wrong?" Connor asked. Ellis looked around, then pulled her hush puppy out of her pocket, flicked it on, and set it on the gameboard in the middle of the lollipop woods. Ilva raised an eyebrow.

"Something happened today." She told them how the mission had ended.

"I see no problem with using such a weapon," Ilva disagreed. "Lola was a murderer and traitor. She brought the ceiling down on herself."

In some ways, Ellis agreed. Lola hadn't just killed Rollo. She had also tried to take over the Homestead in her quest for personal revenge. Ilva had always been hard-headed about revenge, but there was sympathy in Connor's eyes. "I understand Lola's rage, although I no longer share it. I might have walked a similar path, but…"

His eyes landed on Ellis, and she understood. *You had me.* She was his daughter, and she was a human. She had been a moderating force in his life.

Ellis stared thoughtfully at a row of tomato soup cans. "Lola was eager to destroy humanity like the DRI was eager to destroy the drow. I think Sebastian has the same single-minded rigidity, and it's rubbed off on his crew."

"At least Sebastian's goals are reasonable," Ilva countered. "He was right to blow up Marusya Klimova's yacht."

"I was on board!" Ellis protested.

"Would you have wanted to live in a world where Klimova's plan succeeded?" Ilva asked.

"You should be friends with Val," Ellis muttered. "I know you're right, but it makes me uneasy. And even though I sense Sebastian's rigidity and focus, I'm not sure what he wants."

She told them about the tug she'd felt from the ring, the sense that it was pulling her toward the sword. "I'm not sure I should help them. I don't want to become a weapon for a cause I don't understand."

"I respect your hesitation," Connor agreed. "But if the sword in your vision is real, I cannot think of a better person to wield it."

He put his arm around her. Ellis leaned her head on her father's shoulder, reveling in his sturdy support. Her anxiety flowed out of her, and her exhaustion finally relinquished her to sleep.

When Ellis woke up, she was still in the storage bay, lying on a military cot and covered by a thick wool blanket. The game had been packed up. As she sat up, her father appeared from behind a stack of canned food.

"What time is it?" Ellis asked.

"Seven in the morning. How did you sleep?"

She couldn't remember sleeping at all. The hours had passed in a dreamless, enveloping darkness, a nothingness as powerful as the blade of the sword in her vision. "I slept okay, I think. And I know what I want to do."

She didn't have to find Sebastian. He came looking for her a few minutes after she woke up. "Time to carry out your end of the bargain. Trissa's back. Where's the sword?"

Ellis didn't like the my-way-or-the-highway rigidity in his voice, but she'd made her choice.

"I don't know..." she began. Sebastian's eyes got angry, but before he could speak, she explained about the ring and the tug she'd felt while she was wearing it. "It's pulling me somewhere important."

"Toward the sword?"

"I think so."

"Will you put the ring on now? Please?"

She nodded and pulled the ring off the string around her neck. The metal got icy the second it slipped past her knuckle. Adrenaline pumped as she waited to see if the ring would send her another vision. Maybe it was like a VHS tape, and it would have to play the whole vision for her from the start.

She wasn't dropped through another hole in reality, though. A pinprick of restlessness rose in her guts, an interior itch that traveled from her core through her bones before bursting out into the world. Ellis instinctively turned, yielding to the pull. Her hand rose, index finger straightening. "There."

"Are you sure?" the captain asked. "Take your time."

"I don't need time. I'm sure."

Sebastian pulled a compass from his pocket and took a reading, fiddling with it. Then he touched a button on his watch and stared at the small screen for a minute. Wherever she was pointing, it meant something to him.

Finally, Sebastian made a call. "Val. We've got a heading.

Meet me in the map room. You'll never guess where the ring wants us to go."

When he glanced at Ellis, she realized her hand was still in the air, suspended by the ring's magnetic pull. "What do you mean? Where am I pointing?"

He turned without answering, waving her toward the ladder. He took the steps two or three at a time, vibrating with a giddy excitement that only got stronger as they entered the map room at the top of the ship. There was a large circular table covered by a digital display. The ring's pull didn't go away, and Ellis' hand floated up whenever she stopped actively thinking about it.

"Can you do the thing?" Sebastian asked, nodding at Ellis. She stopped fighting the pull and pointed. Sebastian worked with the digital display table, pulling up a map of the California coastline that showed their current position as a large purple dot. After a few taps, a line appeared on the map, matching the direction Ellis was pointing.

"See?" he asked Val.

She whistled, face a grim mask.

"What's going on?" Ellis asked.

As Sebastian turned to her, his expression was hesitant. "I have to tell you something."

"I don't think that's a good idea," Val interjected.

"If we're going to give her an ancient magical sword, we'd better make sure she's on board with our plans first," Sebastian shot back.

"All she *needs* is to do what she's told," Val growled.

Ellis snorted, which caused the other two to look at her with amazement. "Come on, Val," Sebastian protested. "You've been following her as long as I have. Be realistic."

Ellis shivered at the thought of the Violet Eye tracking her movements across the years. It was as unsettling as the memory of Lola's annihilation. Maybe more so, but she needed to know what Sebastian wanted to tell her, and discussing her discomfort with the surveillance might give him pause.

"If you want to stake our whole plan on an untrained out-of-control kid, it's your funeral." Val's lips pressed into a tight line. Whatever Sebastian was going to tell her, the first mate wanted no part of it.

He tapped a button on the table display, and the map of their surroundings zoomed out to show the entire globe. A pop-up window appeared requesting a password, and Sebastian swiftly typed in a long sequence of numbers and letters. When he finished, there was a pleasant beep, and the map lit up with purple dots ranging in size from pinpricks to quarter-sized splotches.

At first, Ellis was unsure of what the dots represented. Then her eyes were drawn to the California coastline, and her heart skipped a beat when she saw the medium-sized dot situated in a familiar stretch of the Angeles National Forest. It was the location of the Swallow's Nest.

Ellis' eyes widened to take in the size and variety of gleaming purple lights. "These are all drow communities!" She tapped a large spot in the middle of the Mongolian desert.

"That's right," Sebastian agreed.

Ellis' pleasure at seeing the map turned to anxiety. The drow had relied on secrecy and concealment to coexist with the much larger human population. The map was awe-inspiring, but it was also dangerous. "You've been using the Violet Eye to locate drow populations."

Sebastian nodded. "We have. It's possible that we've missed a few insular communities, but we know where most of them are." He spread his fingers across the purple-dotted table. "We aren't seeking power for power's sake. We're pursuing a specific goal. We intend to announce the existence of the drow to the world. It's time to leave our troglodytic past behind us and come into the light."

Ellis flinched at the word "light." It was classic human behavior to frame anything bright as good. The drow didn't think that way.

"What you're talking about is incredibly dangerous. You don't know how people will react. For all you know, you're about to start World War Three."

"That's why we need the sword." Sebastian said that too coolly for Ellis' comfort. "We've gotten buy-in from the majority of Homesteads. As the human population grows, it gets harder for the drow to conceal themselves, and we're going to reach a tipping point soon.

"With global communications and independent media, the other shoe could drop at any time. I'm going to seize the narrative to channel the inevitable chaos toward a positive end. Humans and drow *will* live together peacefully."

Ellis tried to count the number of dots on the map. "Even if you have to start a hundred wars?"

"Yes." Sebastian's eyes blazed. He didn't seem to understand the irony of his position, and anxiety burned in her guts.

A vision of DRI soldiers marching toward the Swallow's

Nest armed with lightsilk cannons and automatic weapons surfaced in Ellis' mind. Maybe they wouldn't send a ground unit. The military might bomb first and ask questions later.

Ellis reached for the icy ring, realizing with a start that her hand had floated back into the air. She ripped the metal from her finger and slid it across the digital map. The display flickered where the ring touched it, and Sebastian dove for it before it slid off the table.

"I won't do it," she asserted. "I won't risk my people like that."

"*Your* people? You mean the ones who lined up to wipe your memory? The ones who ostracized you throughout your childhood? Those aren't your people, Ellis. You're smarter than them. You expanded their horizons with the Outpost, but it doesn't have to stop there. My plan will take things a step further. Think of how well-positioned you are to be our ambassador. I know in my gut that it's what Nan Elandra would have wanted."

The words twisted into her, but Ellis pushed the appeal to her beloved grandmother away. Sebastian had the same spark in his eyes she'd seen in Marusya Klimova—and sometimes in her mother. It was a thinly veiled hunger for power and control.

"You'll have to find another half-drow because I won't do it."

"You might change your mind when I tell you where the sword is," Sebastian wheedled.

Val made a low, annoyed noise, but he ignored her and kept talking. "A few days after your assault on the Chiaro Institute, we started picking up radio chatter from the US military. Back-channel intelligence, ultra-top-secret stuff. They picked up a group of people they believed to be involved in the attack. Friends of yours."

He tapped the screen, and a neat grid of four photographs appeared. Ellis focused on the photo on the top left—an unmistakable, if unflattering, image of Charlie Morrissey. Her heart lurched, feet sinking into the floor. "No! That's not possible."

"I'm afraid so. The Army's got your little cop boyfriend."

Ellis was too destabilized to respond to the dig.

"He's dead. Everyone in the Homestead said he was dead!"

"Either they lied to you, or the United States military has perfected the art of necromancy."

Ellis hissed through her teeth. She wanted to fight someone, primarily Lola. Hoping seemed dangerous at the moment. If she let her shell crack and Sebastian was wrong, it might destroy her. "Maybe you're the one who's lying. Why would Charlie and Percy be in the same place as the sword? It's too much of a coincidence."

"It's not a coincidence," Sebastian said. "The DRI was a specialist organization focused on the drow, but it wasn't the military's only secret project. They've taken an interest in Charlie and one other man."

An image of Percy flashed onto the screen, white hair twisting in wild waves above his head. The mug shot made him look old.

"We've been watching a military weapons silo in Southeastern Nevada for years. It's not exclusive to magic weapons. Anything the military deems weird or uncanny winds up there."

"Including people," Val interjected.

Percy and Charlie would be considered uncanny.

"We have to rescue them!" Ellis cried.

"The captain doesn't *have* to do anything," Val snarled.

Sebastian's smile went oily. "I'm a pragmatist, Ellis. I feel for your friends, but taking on the United States military to rescue strangers is not a good use of the *Violet Eel*'s resources. However, if the mission *also* gave us access to, say, an ancient magical sword, things might be different."

"Charlie and Percy are worth a hundred magic swords each. All of them are."

"Not to me, they're not."

His mercenary expression lowered the temperature in the room. "You're a sick bastard," Ellis snapped.

Val straightened to her full height, muscles rippling under her fatigues. "If you don't like it, you can duel the captain for his stripes."

"Screw you!" Ellis exclaimed. "Screw both of you."

She turned and was about to storm off when Sebastian called after her, "Don't forget your ring!" He chuckled and tossed it toward her.

Ellis backed away and let it fall, but a moment later, she clutched the circle of metal in her fingers, the large pearl pressing into her palm. Ellis desperately wanted to fling it back, but she was physically unable. *What the hell?* Her fingers automatically moved to replace the ring on its cord and hang it around her neck. Shivering, she left the map room at a run.

CHAPTER NINETEEN

Charlie had only gotten rough with a suspect twice in his LAPD career. Both times, he'd been ashamed of his behavior, but he couldn't be ashamed of his anger at men who had committed the worst offenses known to humankind.

Sometimes he'd been jealous of dirty cops. Ron Jackson in particular, who knew where all the blind spots in the booking station's cameras were and would beat a suspect senseless, even if it meant losing a conviction. Sometimes he fantasized about surrendering to his anger and accessing its volcanic power.

There was no anger in his current guards. Their cold efficiency made him uneasy. Since the moment they'd removed his blindfold, he'd expected violence, awaiting the day when they would take him to a dank basement instead of the greige tedium of the interrogation room.

Each time his guards handcuffed him, he wondered if today would be the day, so when the bracelets tightened and they added a blindfold, his heart skipped a beat. When they walked him past the hall leading to the interrogation room, he expected nothing good.

Flexing his fingers, he felt for the shadow magic around him. He'd wanted to gather more information before he tried to escape, particularly regarding the whereabouts of his friends, but he didn't think his convictions would hold up in a faceoff with jumper cables. To distract himself, he ran through one of Helene's shadow magic lessons, slowing his breathing and paying attention to his surroundings.

They passed through a set of double doors, and the quality of the sound surrounding him changed. From the echo of the guard's footsteps, Charlie guessed he was in a warehouse. A moment later, a hand roughly shoved him to the floor.

New footsteps approached, their sound so distinctive that Charlie frowned. A woman in heels.

"Hello, Senator," Charlie greeted, hazarding a guess.

He heard a sharp, surprised intake of breath.

"Don't worry," Charlie added, "My blindfold's on plenty tight. I'm not trying to get the men in trouble. It's just that you're the only person in this hole who bothers to wear heels."

"I see why the LAPD prized your deduction skills," Chan replied. She might be making fun of him, but he didn't think so. "I'll get straight to the point, Detective Morrissey. We're all done with carrots. We've decided to break out the stick."

He flexed his fingers, wondering if this was the point at which a big guy with facial scars would connect electrodes to his body. Aside from the firm hand on his shoulder, no one touched him. Chan's heels clicked closer. "Your friend Percy gave us some very interesting information about your nyctophobia."

Nyctophobia? Charlie searched his brain for the word. He didn't have any phobias. Well-founded fears of being shot, sure, but that wasn't irrational. "Nyctophobia. Is that where I'm afraid of guys named Nick?"

"Your wit won't help you in this ordeal, Charlie." She had stopped calling him Detective Morrissey, presumably to reinforce her bad-cop transformation. "And you don't have to be coy. I'm going leave you alone in this storage bay. We have disconnected the electricity, and we are some distance underground, so there is no natural light. The space is quite large, and I suspect, despite your crippling fear of the dark, that you will try to effect an escape."

It clicked then. *Nyctophobia. Fear of night, or more specifically, of the dark.*

Chan had moved on. "Your escape will fail. In two hours, the guards will turn the lights back on. We will do this every day until you tell me everything I want to know about the attack on the Chiaro Institute."

Why would Percy tell them I'm afraid of the dark?

Charlie realized the answer. Percy was deploying reverse psychology against their captors. More importantly, he was letting Charlie know that it was time to act. A boot shoved Charlie onto his side. His hands were still cuffed in front of him, and he listened as the soldiers' and Senator Chan's footsteps receded.

A gut instinct made him sit up and call after them. If Percy had set this up, he could playact to support the lie. *"Please. No! Don't! Don't leave me alone in the dark!"*

"Two hours," Chan called back cheerfully. Then the door slammed, followed quickly by the snick of an electronic lock.

When he was alone, Charlie scrabbled for the blindfold. Chan hadn't lied. The darkness surrounding him was complete. It was rich with shadow magic too, although that wouldn't stop him from tripping over his own feet. Staying on his hands and knees, Charlie felt his way around his immediate surroundings. He threw in some screams and hollers in case someone was listening at the door.

It was possible that his captors were watching him, but as he got a better sense of his surroundings, he thought it unlikely. This was an ordinary storage bay packed with metal shelves and loaded with boxes. The first one he tore open contained bags of flour. Another shelf held aluminum cans.

Senator Chan's plan had flair. Turning off the lights in his cell wouldn't have had nearly the same effect. He knew that space well by now. The uncertain vastness of a storage bay plunged into darkness was much more threatening. Genuine fear rose in Charlie's body as he climbed to his feet and stumbled down an aisle in search of a wall, hands outstretched to protect himself.

They should have put a cave spider in with me. Charlie congratulated himself for thinking of an innovative interrogation technique, but his spirits sank as he wondered if he was really alone. He stopped dead, listening for distinctive eight-legged clicks. He heard only silence, but his fear grew as he continued forward.

When he finally stumbled into a wall, he sank down against it to collect his thoughts and make a plan. This was what he knew: he was imprisoned underground, Percy believed they needed to escape, and his captors didn't know he could do shadow magic.

Charlie might not be able to see, but he had an abundant supply of shadow magic. He couldn't use it without attracting attention, and he'd bet good money that this facility had lightsilk weapons in storage.

One shot. He would get one shot to save himself and his friends.

He would have to use dissolution magic. He still felt horror when he thought about removing matter from the world, but it was nothing compared to the horror of allowing his companions to be permanently held in this sterile pit. Not when Chan and her military backers had shown a willingness to use torture.

Oh, right. This *is supposed to be torture.* Charlie screamed for his mother, allowing a hint of truth to animate his cries. His mother was getting older and currently believed that he was in a top-secret six-month police training program. She wouldn't worry about him yet, but never hearing from him again would crush her.

Start with your cuffs, Charlie. Surely you can dissolve a measly pair of handcuffs.

The problem was that the chain connecting the handcuffs was close to his hands, which Charlie needed for things like filling out police reports in triplicate and someday learning to play the acoustic guitar he'd gotten in Acapulco five years ago.

I won't be learning to play anything if I don't get out of here.

He hadn't used shadow magic since arriving in the facility. He'd been too afraid of giving himself away before he had a plan. He was rusty, but Chan had given him two hours, and he had to make the most of the time.

Go ahead and summon the forces of darkness, Charlie. Try not to slice your fingers off in the process.

Breathing hard, he pulled a globule of shadow magic into his hand. It was hardly bigger than a marble. He wouldn't need much to slice through the chain.

Breathe. Reach out with the magic. And push.

His breath hitched, and he forced it into a steady pattern. It was tricky curving the shadow magic toward the chain, but by holding his arms at right angles, he was able to do it. Before he had time to worry, the globule brushed the metal chain.

Charlie pushed the magic forward, the deep breathing doing nothing to calm his galloping heartbeat. Almost immediately, the metal gave way, and he continued to push until there was a *clink* and the ends of the chain dropped. Sighing in relief, he celebrated his new freedom of movement by swinging his arms in wild loops.

Could he disguise his escape? Make Chan and the soldiers believe he had managed it in some way other than using magic? An idea formed in Charlie's mind. If they thought he was dead, they wouldn't look for him. It had worked in the drow caverns, and it might work here. Charlie felt his way along the wall until he reached a corner. Counting his steps, he paced from there to the next corner—a good forty feet, he guessed. He hoped he would have enough room to bring down the ceiling without killing himself.

Charlie stood in an open spot on the floor near the corner. He was unsteady in the blackness, but he trusted his inner ear. Stretching both hands above his head, he gathered massive balls of shadow magic into his fists, trying to imitate what he'd done when he'd brought the cavern ceiling down in the Homestead. He pulled in whirling shadows until his body was on fire with power and anticipation. Then he sent the magic toward the ceiling in the opposite corner of the storage bay.

He would bring the roof down, then turn invisible and wait for the guards to come back. He hoped they would believe he'd been smashed under the rock. More magic poured out of his fingers into the air. He was almost there.

Just. One. More. Push.

The shadow magic surged forward, but something was very wrong.

Charlie grunted in pain as the magic collided with a fiery, immovable wall. What the hell was happening? He forced himself to press on through the shock, hoping his fear of dissolution magic was playing tricks on him. When a noise came from the ceiling, he thought he'd succeeded, but the *click-click-click* wasn't cracking concrete. It was a mechanical release. *What the hell is that?* His question was answered when a heavy net fell on his head.

It was like having an electric fence flung over his body. The agony was so intense that it took Charlie a moment of desperate fighting to realize what was happening. The balls of magic in his fists had disappeared, leaving him hot and empty. *Lightsilk. DRI lightsilk.*

As Charlie screamed, the overhead lights turned on, and soldiers rushed into the room. Instead of freeing him from the net, they pressed the burning silk down on his skin, which turned him into a bundle of agony and raw nerves. He had a sensation of being carried, and then, to his great relief, he passed out.

When Charlie woke, he was still in pain. The full-body ache felt like a blistered sunburn, and his bare skin was covered with welts. The soldiers had moved him to a new cell that had lightsilk netting across the bars. His heart raced and he shied away, crying out as the concrete scraped the burned skin of his back. When this new agony subsided, he reached for a plastic water bottle that had been left on the floor.

"How'd you sleep?" a stern voice asked. Senator Chan was standing outside his cell, figure fuzzed by the netting.

"Fuck off," Charlie snarled.

She ignored his insult. "You didn't waste any time falling into our trap."

"How did you know what would happen?" he asked, too exhausted to trade barbs. He gingerly laid back on the concrete and stared at the ceiling.

"Oh, please. 'Charlie's afraid of the dark'? Percy Rawlings would never throw his friends under the bus like that. The loyalty would be admirable if you lot weren't so intent on disrupting critical national research projects. I admit, you put on a pretty good show, screaming and hollering about the lights. Begging not to be thrown into the nasty briar patch. Very summer stock."

"What are you going to do now?"

"First, you're going to write a complete autobiography."

"Surely a senator from the great state of California can pull my LAPD file. You already know what happened at the DRI."

"Don't be cute. I need to know where you acquired your dark magic abilities."

"I don't know what you're talking about."

"I guess your handcuffs fell off by themselves."

"They were rusty," Charlie shot back sullenly.

"I can arrange another encounter with lightsilk if you'd like your newfound powers confirmed." She ran one French-manicured nail over the net. Charlie shivered as it rippled in the light. "I didn't think so." Chan paced for a moment, then stopped. "You're clearly in pain right now. Take the day to recover. Tomorrow, you can start sharing your personal history."

Charlie stared at the mottled gray ceiling. He hoped it wasn't the last thing he would ever see.

CHAPTER TWENTY

Ellis stormed away without a destination in mind. She feared that if she slowed down, she might be consumed by her rage, so she made two full circles of the ship on the deck before Jerel found her. He was out of breath. "Sorry to interrupt."

"Whatever you need can wait. I'm not in the mood," Ellis shot back.

He was so uneasy that she softened. "What is it?"

"Your friend Trissa. She's awake."

Ellis was off like a shot, taking the steps on the nearest ladder three at a time. She slowed as she reached the medical bay's swinging doors, although her entrance was still frenzied enough to startle the staff. Trissa sat up in a bed on the far side of the room.

"Triss!" Ellis ran toward her friend. She halted at the bedside, not wanting to dislodge any medical equipment.

"Ellis, I have to tell you..."

Ellis cut her off with a gentle hug.

"Has someone gone to get Landon?" she shouted to the

room. Dr. Moray assured her that her brother was on Jerel's errand list.

"Your new potion worked fantastically well," Ellis continued excitedly, words tripping over one another. "Dad made some tweaks. I'm sure he'll bore you with the details. I've been able to use my shadow magic without pain."

Trissa beamed and weakly squeezed Ellis' hand. "That's wonderful, but you've got to shut up while I tell you something extremely important. Charlie is alive."

Ellis went still as the words left Trissa's mouth. Sebastian had said the same thing, but she hadn't believed him. He was too self-interested to trust. Trissa, on the other hand...

"What happened?" Ellis asked. Trissa muddled her way through an explanation. It was a ruse that had gotten out of control. An attempt to lower Lola's guard.

Trissa apologized profusely for not telling Ellis immediately. "I thought I'd get to you before the news, but things got out of control."

"It's okay." Ellis' heartbeat pounded in her ears. "The important thing is that he's alive."

His being alive complicated the situation since it meant Sebastian might be telling the truth about the military detention facility. If Charlie was alive and in captivity, Ellis had to rescue him, but she couldn't shake the sense of being a pawn in Sebastian's schemes.

"What's wrong?" Trissa asked.

Ellis didn't want to burden her. Not yet, anyway. She told Trissa what she knew about the power struggles at the Homestead. Trissa was relieved to hear that the elders were fighting to regain control, and she took the news of Lola's death somberly.

Trissa was reluctant to talk about her time as Lola's captive but sketched an outline of their terrifying flight. Trissa had clearly expected Lola to kill her and was still deeply shaken.

"What are they going to do with Irving?" she asked, looking at the next bed. He'd reacted badly to whatever was in the darts, possibly a side effect of the DRI's experiments, so he was in a medically induced coma. It was just like Trissa to think of others before herself.

They spoke for a few more minutes, with Ellis struggling to explain details about the *Violet Eel*. She desperately wanted to consult Trissa about her dilemma with the ring and the sword, but she didn't trust the doctors in the medical bay to keep her confidence. Moreover, Landon rushed in the door, and her hope of a serious conversation died.

Connor and Ilva followed a few minutes later to check on Trissa and ask if they could be of service. Trissa congratulated Connor on brewing the potion that had renewed Ellis' shadow magic, and Ellis zoned out as the conversation veered to the alchemical.

As she sat on Trissa's bed, surrounded by the people who loved her most in the world, Ellis felt her shell cracking. Lola had lied. Charlie was alive. The sadness she'd worked so hard to contain flooded out of her, and it was all she could do to keep her head above the surface.

"Ellis? *Ellis*?" An insistent voice pulled Ellis back to shore, and she blinked.

"Is everyone okay?" she asked.

"We're all right," Landon replied. "Are you? You sure the old farts didn't wipe your memory?"

Connor sharply rebuked his son, but Ellis smiled. It was nice to see Landon joking. "Trissa, I'm sorry to pull the focus, but you all are my family, and I need to ask for your help. Can you cast a muffling spell?" she asked. When Connor did so, she related her conversation with Sebastian in detail. She explained about his plan to integrate humans and drow and told them about Charlie's captivity.

When she was done, her father's face was stonier than usual. "I wish I had met the young man earlier in his life. I can't imagine Mother would have approved of this."

Ellis was inclined to agree. "I don't trust him. The only reason I believe him even a little is that Trissa confirmed that Charlie is alive. He seemed quite certain of that, and if there's any chance that he's telling the truth, I have to try to save them."

"Of course you do." Ilva nodded.

Ellis smiled gratefully. "I wish I didn't have to ask, but..."

"We're coming with you," Landon interjected.

"I..."

Landon waved his hand. "I shouldn't speak for everyone. *I'm* coming with you."

"So am I," Connor interjected.

"I can hardly allow my son and my... I can hardly allow my *family* to go into battle without me," Ilva added.

"Neither can I," Trissa affirmed.

"Triss, I'm not going to drag you out of your hospital bed to go on a secret mission."

"I wouldn't go if I thought I'd bring you down.

According to Doc, I reacted badly to the darts because I was malnourished and dehydrated, but I'll be right as rock by tomorrow."

"It's going to be dangerous," Ellis warned.

"When has that *ever* kept us away?" Connor drawled.

When Ellis went to speak to Sebastian about retrieving the sword, she was not alone. Her family marched into Sebastian's quarters as a unit, interrupting an intense conversation with Val.

"To what do I owe the pleasure of this family reunion?" he asked. His smirk suggested he knew the answer.

"I'll go get your sword," Ellis said without preamble. "But I have conditions."

"I've given you a lot of leeway," Sebastian countered. "However, I'm the captain of this ship, and I give the orders."

"Not if you want me to play King Arthur, you don't," Ellis shot back.

Her insistence angered him, but she had him over a barrel, and he finally sighed. "What do you want, Your Majesty?"

"I want to lead the raid on the military silo," Ellis announced.

"Absolutely not."

Ellis ignored him. "*My* team will rescue my friends first. *Then* we'll go after your sword."

Sebastian threw up his hands. "Val will lead the raid. She has the right experience."

"So do I," Ellis snapped. "I've saved the world at least as many times as she has."

"You don't know what you're asking," Sebastian warned. "You don't know anything about the silo."

"I said I would lead the raid, not that I would stupidly reject your help. I'm happy to consider your intelligence. Besides, the more you do to help me rescue Charlie and the others, the stronger I'll be when I go for the sword."

"I don't think this is a good idea," Val warned.

Ellis glared at her. "You can think anything that manages to penetrate your dense skull, but if you want the sword, you have to follow my lead."

Val started to respond but stopped when Sebastian put a hand on her arm. "You've gotta be kidding me!" she exclaimed when she saw his face.

Sebastian shook his head. "I'm not. This is our shot at the sword, and I'm taking it."

"Good." Ellis nodded. "Now, tell me everything you know."

CHAPTER TWENTY-ONE

The military's top-secret weapons bunker was not Fort Knox. It was much *more* secure. The surface entrance was heavily guarded, with automatic gun turrets and constant patrols. The silo was composed of multiple layers separated by airlocks, any of which could be sealed and deoxygenated by soldiers on the surface or the other levels.

Sebastian and Val believed Charlie and the others were being held on the third level. The weapons were probably stored deeper. Even with its advanced telecommunications, the *Violet Eel* had struggled to gather comprehensive intelligence. "Whatever's down there, the military *really* doesn't want us to know about it," Sebastian imparted.

Ellis had tested her magic ring a few different times since the captain had agreed to her plan. They took the van on long drives up the Pacific Coast Highway, stopping every so often to confirm compass readings. Ellis, who hadn't been out of Los Angeles much, enjoyed the view of the shoreline, even as the ring consistently tugged her toward the Nevada border. No matter where they drove, the ring pointed her at the silo.

There was one saving grace. The silo was underground. Ellis laughed when she realized how simple the solution was. *If they wanted to protect their fancy weapons from drow, they should have stored them in a tower.*

"I just don't see how we're going to fight our way through more than three floors of military resistance." Val grimaced. They were in the map room, huddled around the digital display table.

"We're not going to fight," Ellis stated. "We're going to walk in the back door."

"What do you mean? What back door?"

"The back door we dig." Ellis grinned. Okay, not *dig*. The drow had never bothered inventing the shovel.

"You're talking about thousands of feet of rock," Val protested.

"That's right," Ellis agreed. "The drow have done it before, and we can do it again."

Neither Val nor Sebastian was a shadow mage, so Ellis thought they might object to her plan. Neither did, further proof that the security situation in the silo was dire. A moment after Ellis spoke, Val climbed to her feet, stretched her limbs, and headed to the door.

"Come on, Val! It's a good plan," Sebastian called.

"It's not a *good* plan, but I'll grant you it's the *only* plan," Val agreed.

"So, where are you going?"

"To send the scout team to find us a place to drop the shaft. Believe it or not, the military isn't full of blind idiots.

We can't just show up half a mile out in the desert with a bunch of drilling equipment."

"Thanks, Val," Ellis called. Val ignored her appreciative smile and pushed through the doors harder than she needed to.

Ellis' family made an excellent war cabinet. Connor and Ilva knew more than she did about the practicalities of major tunneling, and so Ellis put them in charge of planning that aspect of the mission. One by one, they interviewed the ship's shadow mages. Ellis had suggested using the *Violet Eel*'s dissolution magic grenades for part of the work, but Sebastian had discouraged her. They were burst weapons, he insisted, poorly suited to the kind of consistent effort they'd need to plunge a shaft into the ground.

A few minutes after Val left, Rami came in with trays of sandwiches and iced tea. He'd never let her forget meals.

"Who does the provisioning for the ship?" Ellis asked.

"I do the planning, and Emily does the buying," he said. "Considering my complexion, I can't march into a warehouse with a shopping list."

Ellis nodded. "All right. I need you two to work together on a special provisioning project. It would be great to have a store of tunnel bars if you can manage it."

"What flavor?" Rami asked with a grin.

"They come in *flavors?*" Ellis asked, astonished.

"They do on the *Violet Eel*."

The bars she'd had in the past had not tasted bad, but they hadn't been exciting, either. She wasted several minutes interrogating Rami about the options, unable to wrap her mind around his recommendation, which was blueberry milkshake.

"How many do you need?" he asked.

"That's what I need you to tell me." Ellis relayed the plan.

When she took her first bite of a blueberry milkshake tunnel bar, Ellis regretted letting Rami strong-arm her into the choice. She could taste the blueberry. She could even taste the milkshake, but below both was that unmistakable fungal tunnel-bar funk. It was only slightly more disgusting than it was comforting.

"Have you rested sufficiently?" Ilva asked. Dirt streaked her purple skin, and beads of sweat made soft noises as they dripped off her face onto the rock. Ellis retrieved a sturdy metal canister from her belt, took a sip, and wiped her mouth, feeling a burst of pleasure as her shadow magic renewed itself.

"Sure have." Ellis carefully climbed down the slope around Ilva. It was possible to pass other people in the tunnel if you were both careful. They'd kept the shaft narrow to conserve energy.

They had opted to tunnel into the silo at a sharp angle. As Ellis climbed down the nearly forty-five-degree shaft, she slipped the black ring onto her finger. The tension constricting her guts released at the ring's familiar tug.

Ellis hadn't told anyone that she now felt the tug even when she wasn't wearing the ring. The sensation wasn't the same. When she wore the ring, its pull was physical. When it was in her pocket, its attraction was mental. Part of her mind was constantly with the ring, the black metal band chewing at her thoughts. It was alarming, but for now, she needed Sebastian focused on finding Charlie, not distracted by novel information about his favorite magic ring.

Ellis took her spot at the rock wall and raised her hands. She was ashamed to admit that she wanted to blast straight through rock to the sword. Since she was wearing the ring, there was nothing to distract her from imagining gripping the blade's hilt and wielding its slicing edge against the world.

"Ellis?" someone said, shaking her from her reverie.

"Yes! I'm here!" She forced her attention back to the task. She didn't have time to be disturbed by the increasingly vivid fantasies the ring encouraged since she had rock to annihilate.

For a while, she lost herself in the repetitive work. She was a cog in the assembly line and fell into a comfortable rhythm. Gather magic, spin it into a disc, and push it forward until the rock in front of her disappeared. Step forward, gather, spin, and push again. Step, gather, spin, push. Sweat beaded on her forehead, chilled by the cool earth. Her constant descent seemed to satisfy the ring.

When her shadow magic became shiftier and less easy to control, Ellis stopped and sipped the potion. Renewed, she returned to her labors for another hour. When Connor touched her shoulder, Ellis half-jumped out of her skin.

"Are you all right?" he asked.

Ellis didn't realize she was pointing until he looked in that direction and, embarrassed, lowered her hand. "I'm fine. We're getting closer."

"You're a little off-target," Connor inspected her latest

stretch of tunnel. Under her watch, it was almost a vertical shaft.

"Sorry." Ellis stared in the direction she'd been tunneling. A spark of energy traveled from her index finger to her core, and it took all her willpower not to spend the wild excess dissolving more rock. "I can feel it down there," she murmured. Connor looked at where she was pointing. *When did that happen?*

Connor said something inconsequential and gently moved around her toward the open tunnel face, squeezing her shoulder as he went. "You should rest. We're only a few hours out."

Ellis yanked the ring off her finger and slipped it back onto a long chain around her neck, closing the clasp with shaking hands. Landon spoke to her as she walked past him, but she had trouble seeing him as real. At least half of her attention was on the ring, and she played with the chain as she climbed the slope.

Most of her team was sitting a few hundred feet up in a low-ceilinged cavern Ilva had hollowed out as a rest area. As they shifted to make room for Ellis, she slumped against the wall, realizing she hadn't thought about Charlie for hours. She tried to imagine his face but quickly gave up and went back to fiddling with the ring.

Maybe I should go for the sword first. The thought jolted her out of her complacency. She had to stay sharp. Charlie first, then the sword. If she let her guard down, her feet might carry her away from him. She couldn't let that happen.

She would try to nap. In the darkness behind her eyelids, a black metal circle blazed, empty and cold, circumscribing an endless void. Ellis let herself fall into the void, but her dreams were fitful.

Trissa woke her, putting a hand on Ellis' head to stop her from slamming it into the low ceiling.

"Are we there?" Ellis asked. Her mouth tasted like spider dung.

"No."

"Then why did you wake me up?" Ellis spat, viciousness welling up from a part of her that still wanted to sleep.

"I…" Trissa scratched her chin and pulled her knees to her chest. "You didn't look like you were asleep. You looked like you were in another world. It scared me."

She handed Ellis a tunnel bar and a large plastic water bottle by way of apology. Ellis took a bite and grimaced. Blueberry milkshake.

As it turned out, Trissa was wrong. They *were* close. They made their first incursion into the silo minutes later.

It was more or less an accident. Ilva was taking her turn at tunneling, and she was working on three feet of rock that turned to be two feet of rock and one of concrete. This information traveled back through the tunnel in shouts, and Ellis clambered down the steep passage to look at the concrete.

Ellis ran a hand over the uneven seam between the concrete and the rock, considering her next move. "Do we have a precise location?"

Connor shook his head. "Probably the second silo level."

"I wish we could do better than probably, but we'll make it work."

They'd been working like dogs to clear the tunnel. Even

Landon, who was not a strong shadow mage, had taken a turn. They needed somewhere to rest and maybe even retreat. Ellis pointed at Ilva. "Clear out a staging room fifty feet up the tunnel. Leave it narrow, though, so we can cave it in if we have to. Let's get everyone down here. In the meantime, let's take a look at the part of the building we hit."

Ilva went off to hollow out their staging area while Rami climbed up the passage to rally their forces in the nearest rest pocket. Under Ellis' direction, Trissa spun out a thin tendril of shadow magic and drilled a tiny hole in the concrete just large enough for a fiberoptic camera. When it snaked through the hole, it showed a storage bay —a big concrete box stuffed with wire shelves of canned goods. One of the rows had been disturbed—the racks tipped over, and their contents spilled across the floor. Dented cans, mostly, but there was a fair amount of flour as well.

"What happened there? An accident?" Ellis asked. The black metal ring, nestled in the hollow of her throat, got very cold. It burned her skin until Ellis yanked it off its chain and slid it back on her finger.

Yes-yes-yes! The metal vibrated with excitement, then stilled, cold but no longer painful. Ellis was giddy. She was so close. If she could just wrap up a few pesky chores first. What was it she was supposed to do? A rescue? Faces floated into her mind, those of a stocky brown-haired man and a woman with long hair that rippled in red waves like a forest fire. Ellis couldn't put names to those faces. She couldn't think about anything but the ring. The tug had become insistent, direct, and urgent. She was certain the sword was beneath her feet, deeper in the silo. *I'm coming. I'm coming.*

"I don't know," Sebastian muttered, interrupting her train of thought.

"You don't know what?"

"Why the storage racks are messed up. Maybe a soldier knocked them over with a forklift."

Ellis glanced at Sebastian's handheld screen. His information was incomplete, but it would have to do. Staring at the small night vision monitor, Sebastian tapped the beady security cameras in the corners of the room.

"The coverage is good but not complete." He pointed out two blind spots. "If we go in through a small hole in the wall in the near corner, the cameras won't see us."

Ellis nodded. "Make it happen." She laid her forehead against the concrete. She was *so* close, and if she punched through the wall, she'd be closer.

"Ellis!" Sebastian barked.

She looked down and saw shadow magic twisting in her hands. She didn't remember collecting it. Trissa's potion had almost worn off, but unconsciously, she had collected a few wisps of dark power. Ellis dismissed the magic.

"What's going on?" Sebastian asked.

"Nothing," Ellis lied.

"It's the ring, isn't it?" His eager expression filled Ellis with distrust, which pried her attention loose.

"Get the tunnel in place," she ordered.

Sebastian gave Trissa directions about creating the tunnel, and Ellis went to find her father in the staging area. Halfway there, she stopped and uncorked the bottle of shadow magic potion, gulping the cool liquid. Her senses roared to life, and the shadows of the tunnel pressed thickly around her, goading her.

Connor was the tallest member of the strike force, and when he stood up straight, the top of the staging area grazed his head. The pull of the ring had burned away Ellis' usual uneasiness in cramped spaces, and she felt a surge of pride as her team circled close. Jerel was checking satchels of drow and human medical equipment as the others donned weapons and adjusted their clothing.

Sebastian had outfitted the strike force in tactical light armor made from crystal silk woven onto a carbon nanofiber mesh. He called the fabric "three-strike taffeta" because the clothing would hold up to approximately three bullets. He had offered Ellis a bandolier of dissolution grenades, but she had turned him down. She told herself she didn't want to use a weapon that could annihilate a person, but in reality, she couldn't imagine holding any weapon but the sword. She would be with it soon. *Soon, I promise.*

The ring twitched, and Ellis took it as a sign to start the meeting. "We will keep this mission covert as long as possible. Cloakers on. Hush puppies on. Once we're through the tunnel, we'll cover it back up and send out a scouting party to look for the sword."

There was a murmur of surprise at the change in plans. Ellis' brain fogged for a minute, and then she shook her head. "Sorry, I mean. Once we're through the tunnel, we'll go look for...ugh, what's his name? Brown hair. Former cop?"

"Charlie?" Landon asked incredulously. Less observant

than his parents or Trissa, he hadn't picked up on Ellis' disorientation.

"You're not fit to lead this mission," Sebastian told her quietly. If there had been a hint of cruelty or elation in his voice, Ellis would have dismissed the statement, but Sebastian had not questioned Ellis' orders since he'd ceded control of the mission. He was a dogged asset, working tirelessly to support Ellis' decisions. His withering assessment of Ellis' fitness was clipped and professional.

"I…I…" As Ellis stammered, Ilva sucked in a breath. Ellis' body had twisted, and both her hands now pointed down. When had she put the ring back on? Ellis tore it from her finger, sweaty and panting. "Something's happening."

"You're sick," Sebastian reluctantly agreed. "That's it. I'm taking control of this mission back."

"No! The mission hasn't changed. Only…I'm going for the sword." Ellis' voice was too loud for the space. Everything was too sharp, too loud, too dense. When she had the sword, she could cut through the noise.

"We should carry out the original plan," Connor corrected.

"I-I can't." Her sweat poured onto the cavern floor in a river. "I don't have a choice. I have to go for the sword," she half-shouted, and before anyone could stop her, she vacuumed shadow magic into her hands and sent it into the rock just beyond her feet. *There.* She needed to go *there.* At her neck, the ring vibrated, physically floating off her neck as if pulled by a magnetic force, pointing her deeper into the ground.

"Stop that!" Ilva scolded.

Ellis couldn't stop. She blasted the rock again, hands refilling with shadow magic more quickly than she used it. The power poured out of her as if she were little more than a conduit. "Go. Rescue Charlie," she ordered, voice scratchy and desperate.

"We're not leaving you like this," Landon told her.

"Yes, you are!"

"What is your plan? What are you going to do?" Connor asked as Ellis blasted the rock at her feet again. She had created a good ten feet of tunnel, and there was no sign of her magic ebbing.

"I'm going to do what I have to do," Ellis replied. "I can't stop it. I'm going to get the sword."

"I'll go with you," Sebastian's eyes were gleaming, his pupils dark, cold circles.

"No, you won't. This is my mission. You're going to go get...*shit*."

"Charlie," Trissa supplied. She ran her hand over her satchel of potions, trying to find one that might pull Ellis out of her mania. Landon reached for his sister's shoulder, but she screamed at him not to touch her. She was dissolving rock faster than she ever had in her life, and she was afraid that if someone tried to stop her, she would dissolve them too.

Ellis struggled to corral her racing thoughts. "Charlie. Go for Charlie and the others. I'll go for the sword by myself."

"No, you won't. I'm coming with you," Connor announced. The ring didn't object, and the thought was comforting.

Ellis let out her breath in a sigh. "Yes. *Yes*. Everyone else, go now. I'll find my way back to you." More magic poured through her hands. Her concentration was too intense to hear the orders Sebastian issued to her team, but after a few moments, they carefully moved around her on their march back to the storage bay.

Now that she had stopped fighting the ring, everything got easier. With the cold metal as a compass, she made the rock at her feet disappear. When she hit concrete thirty feet down, Ellis stopped the flow of magic and scrambled down the tunnel. Her father followed without protest.

"What's your plan?" he asked, breathing hard. The tunnel walls were smooth, and Ellis climbed down by bracing her back and legs against the sides of the shaft.

Ellis shook her head. She was way past plans. The air had a metallic smell, and Ellis chimney-climbed faster. A residual sense of self-preservation made her flick on her cloaker and hush puppy, and when she heard her father do the same, her hand rose, and she blasted through the final three feet of concrete in a single dark stream.

Letting go of the wall, Ellis let herself fall and landed on a concrete floor ten feet below with a thud. She had used so much magic on her final push that she had burned a foot-deep hole in the concrete. It wasn't subtle, but Ellis was beyond that. The air so close to the sword was thick and metallic. She sniffed it like a bloodhound, struggling to take in her surroundings. It all seemed meaningless. An electronic lock here, a blast door there. The buzz of fluorescent tubes overhead.

She was in a circular room several hundred feet in diameter. After her father dropped down beside her, he turned in a circle, mouth open in surprise.

The sword was here. She knew it. The ring jerked her into the dimly lit interior of the chamber. She was getting closer. Yes.

"Wait!" Connor called. She ignored him, focusing on her target. The thick metal doors dotting the silo's perimeter reminded Ellis of school lockers, but these lockers were made of thick titanium guarded by electronic locks. Visually, they were all the same, but there was only one that mattered. Energetically unique, it called to Ellis. It wanted her, reeling her in across the floor.

"This must be where they keep their weapons and artifacts," Connor whispered, stopping beside her. Ellis hardly heard him over the buzzing in her ears. Feeling as weightless as a bolt of lightning, she moved toward the door that burned brightly in her vision.

"Slow d—" Before her father could finish his warning, she was gone. Her focus was so narrow that she wouldn't have seen the guards if they hadn't walked directly in front of her twenty feet away. Ellis slowed her pace, although she couldn't bring herself to stop. Her cloaker and hush puppy held strong, and the soldiers didn't look back as she put her hands on the titanium.

Her father caught up with her. "In a few minutes, those guards will see the hole we made in their ceiling."

"It doesn't matter," Ellis whispered, putting her head against the metal. The pull from the ring was so intense that Ellis felt like she could put her hand through the solid metal. Surely, the magnetic force between the sword and ring would pull the atoms of her hand through the empty spaces in the metal's crystal structure.

Ellis gulped more potion, ignoring her father's protests

about dosage, and dissolved the door. Her brain screamed in triumph as she annihilated the metal, surging forward so quickly that the last tendrils of magic almost cut her fingers. She was insensible of the red light that went off above the vault and the alarm that rang through the vast chamber.

"Ellis!" Her father ducked into the envelope of her cloaker. "We've got to go."

It was like telling her to stop breathing. Ellis ignored him as her eyes devoured the contents of the vault. Had she expected gold and jewels in addition to the sword? There was nothing like that. The only thing inside was a large metal box constructed of several types of dark metal.

"Is that it?" Connor asked.

"It's the right size."

The box had no handles or hinges, only an ornate line that curved down the center on four sides. It was mesmerizing, and Ellis traced it with one finger. The ring was thrilled.

Her father insistently tugged on her arm, and his urgency finally penetrated her brain. Ellis scooped up the ornate box and allowed him to pull her away. Its proximity to the sword sated the ring…for now.

Rudderless, Ellis allowed her father to pull her away from the sounds of footsteps rushing toward the flashing red alarm.

"They have not found our tunnel yet," Connor told her. The guards who had passed them a moment earlier had run back to check on the alarm. "We could go back the way we came and rejoin our party on Level Three."

Ellis had a sudden urge to open every door in the vault

and steal the military's precious treasures like they had stolen her friends.

"I don't like the idea of being trapped in a narrow tunnel. If they find either end, we won't stand a chance," Ellis countered. "We could stay cloaked and sneak up two levels. Rejoin the party that way."

"What about the airlocks between the levels?"

"We can cut through an airlock as easily as we cut through rock."

The ring was no longer absorbing her attention. Ellis knew she had to use this moment of clarity. There was no time to waffle over decisions.

"Let's find the door and get out of here." She pulled her father into the center of the room. "I don't like our chances in a small-diameter vertical tunnel."

"Very well." Connor strode toward the hole in the floor.

"Dad! Did you hear me?" Ellis whispered, trotting to keep up with him.

"Yes." He was already gathering shadow magic. Ellis' skin crawled with anticipation. The longer they were in this room, the more time the enemy's forces would have to find them. Before she could object, her father flung the magic, concentrating as it poured into the mouth of the shaft.

Rock rumbled overhead, then cracked. The soldiers who had run to the pilfered vault shouted in alarm, but they were too far away to tell what was happening. After a moment, rocks and dust rained onto the floor.

"There. They can't access our exit tunnel from here," Connor announced. When the rain of pebbles ebbed, Ellis understood that he had caved in their tunnel.

"If things go badly, *we* won't be able to access our exit tunnel."

"Then we must ensure that things go well," Connor replied gravely.

The circular room was so large that it took them a few minutes to find the door, which was almost identical to the featureless gray vaults lining the perimeter. The electronic locks were no match for dissolution magic, and after listening at the door, she and her father slipped into the hall outside.

They nearly ran headfirst into a lightsilk net. The threads were so thin, and it extended so seamlessly from the walls that only a last-minute grab at Connor's collar saved them. Beyond the glittering threads, the door to a large freight elevator opened, and six armored soldiers emerged with their guns raised. Ellis hoped they would have to remove the net to get through the hallway, but they pulled it open in the center where several layers of netting overlapped. Ellis and her father plastered themselves against the wall, and the soldiers passed so close that the air disturbance ruffled the hair on her forearms. Half their jargon was unfamiliar, and their barked conversation reached Ellis in snippets.

"Level Three… Meant as a distraction… Drilling equipment… Prisoners…"

What about the prisoners?

After a tense moment, they passed out of hearing range.

"How do we get through the lightsilk?" Ellis mused, more for herself than anyone. If Connor lost access to his shadow magic, it would seriously hamper their mission.

When Ellis stepped toward the net to investigate their

options, the box clutched under her left arm vibrated. It started as such a low rumble that at first, Ellis thought there was another cave-in elsewhere in the facility. As she neared the net, she realized the box was shaking with pent-up energy. The ring on Ellis' finger was cold again.

"It wants out," she whispered. Connor had stayed against the wall, and her hush puppy muffled her words.

Ellis put her hands on the box, and there was an answering call from inside. Sinking into a cross-legged position, Ellis laid her palms on the top.

What do you want?

The box jolted on her lap. She searched the etched metal for a catch but found nothing. It was very old, so Ellis was reluctant to blast it open, but she was also deep underground in a military weapons silo with no clear exit. She hoped the drow who had forged the box would understand. Ellis sent an experimental thread of shadow magic toward the box. When it touched the metal, it rebounded with a jolt, hitting her and causing a fiery blossom of pain.

That's new.

Ellis went to the etching around the box's perimeter. The gray band was flush with the darker metal, but it seemed different, not just a different color but a different material. *I wonder.* Steeling herself for another jolt, Ellis sent out a tendril of magic. When it touched the gray band, Ellis pushed, and a pinhole appeared.

Then she understood. It was a test. The twisting gray band could be dissolved, but the darker metal could not, and there was very little room to work. The gray band was less than a quarter of an inch wide, and her cuts would have to be very precise if she wanted to avoid shocks.

Grinning in triumph, Ellis began to carve, but her elation made her sloppy. Before she had gotten two inches, her shadow magic bumped the darker metal.

This time, the pain left her nearly insensible. Ellis jerked away so hard that she slammed her head into the wall. She barely noticed the impact because cold fire was spreading across her skin and pricking at her eyes, leaving her blind with pain. The agony ebbed after a moment, but the fear did not.

If she touched the black metal again, it would kill her. The information appeared in her brain in a moment of cold conviction. There would be no third chance, and she cursed herself for squandering the first two. Ellis put the box down, and it jolted in protest. She flicked off her hush puppy. "Dad. Over here."

Her father joined her within the radius of her cloaker. She showed him what she'd discovered, although she downplayed the seriousness of that second magical jolt.

"You should wait to open it until we're somewhere more secure." He glanced at the lightsilk. "We have the cloakers and the hush puppies. If I lose my shadow magic for a time, it's no great problem."

"No. I have to open the box now. I'm not sure why, but I do. It...it *wants* to be opened."

"We know very little about this weapon, and it might not have your best interests at heart. It might not have *anyone's* best interests at heart." Connor eyed the box.

The part of her mind that understood he was right stood no chance against the pull of the sword. Breathing deeply, Ellis re-focused on the box. "It doesn't matter. This is happening. I need my full attention. Please watch over me."

She sent a thread at the carved line, guiding her magic with surgical precision. She meant to take frequent breaks, but after she started, she found it difficult to stop. The box spurred her forward harder the farther she got. As well as she could, she resisted its demands. An intricate spiral design in the center of the longest edge was the worst, and Ellis nearly slipped twice. Then she was on the side where the band was flat and completed that in seconds. Her excitement surged. *I might actually be able to do this.* As Ellis sent her magic curving around the corner, however, there was more noise from the direction of the elevator.

"You should take a break," Connor anxiously faced the end of the hall.

It was a wise suggestion, and Ellis tried to dispel her magic. However, something in the box's interior was holding the other end of the violet tendril of power and wouldn't let go. Ellis' only option was to move forward. "I *can't* stop."

Sweat poured from her face onto the box, where it froze in crystalline lumps. Connor could see from her face that this was not mere stubbornness but some kind of enchantment. He carefully responded. "Then continue, and I will protect you."

Dividing her attention would kill her, so she put herself in her father's hands. Only snippets of the outside world intruded on her bubble of concentration, but it was impossible not to see the shapes moving past her. If one of the incoming stepped sideways and touched the box…

No. She pushed the potential for catastrophe out of her

mind, narrowing her focus to a needle-thin point of shadow magic.

"Something's wrong," someone said. The speaker was a few feet away, and his voice was unfamiliar. "It's cold in here."

Shit. Some humans could sense shadow magic, an evolutionary adaptation to balance the power differential. Ellis desperately hoped the soldier was just spooked.

"Get the pom-pom," another soldier ordered. Ellis would have laughed, but as she tore her focus away from the box, she saw a man pull a shaggy ball of string the size of a Pomeranian out of his utility belt.

Yep, that was a pom-pom. And it was made of lightsilk.

Rah-fucking-rah.

A noise in the distance interrupted Ellis' terror, a whooping shout like a simulated bird call. She recognized the voice. What the hell was her father doing?

The men froze, but then someone barked orders. There was a purple blur, and chaos erupted. Ellis' life depended on her remaining still, and she battled the urge to fight.

When she saw an armored soldier tumble toward her, she knew it was over. The man was barely outside the envelope of her cloaker, and she waited breathlessly for the disruption that would send her magic fatally careening into the dark metal.

When she could feel the soldier's body heat, a hand yanked him away and sent him flying toward one of his brothers-in-arms. Connor had leapt into the fray with wild abandon, shouting at the top of his lungs.

Why did he turn off his cloaker? When she saw him run

down the hall with a whoop, she understood. He was drawing them off.

There was only a six-inch stretch to go, but it was a tricky lace pattern. Had the gray band narrowed, or was it her imagination? Ellis returned to her task as her father took the fight into the distance, pushing her magical needle through a twisting curve and a series of crenelations. *One more arc.* The action came back toward her, and Ellis rushed through the final stretch. Snipping the last millimeter of material holding the box together, Ellis felt its hold on her shadow magic drop, and she dismissed the thread with a gasp of relief.

Her hands moved by instinct to grip the box's lid. She pulled, but nothing happened. Ellis realized she could slide the lid to the side. The intricate puzzle box separated cleanly, revealing a black velvet interior and a blacker metal scabbard.

The sword. The ring pulled her hand toward the hilt. Ellis forced it to freeze for a moment but gave up her resistance at a shout of pain from her father.

The hilt snapped into her hand like a perfectly machined part, and the sword sprang free of its case. The scabbard was made of the same black metal as the ring, and when Ellis gripped it to pull the blade free, the metal burned her hand.

The sword, the sword, the sword. A primal line of communication ran between the ring and the hilt, and Ellis held the blade aloft. It was hard to see the black blade. It was even hard to look at it directly. It was a moving gash in the fabric of the universe, not slicing so much as sucking anything in its path into a separate dimension. When she swung it at the back of a soldier advancing on her father with his automatic rifle raised, it felt unreal. The blade hovered in the air, and when he saw it, Connor looked horrified. Then it fell in total silence.

Her father gasped. Ellis had sliced the soldier and his gun in half.

Oh, shit.

The shadow blade was clean. It annihilated blood as well as bone, which was just as well. You couldn't wipe down a blade that didn't exist.

Another soldier stared at the carnage a second too long, and Ellis put a boot in his face. As she made contact, a silent rebuke from the sword shot through her spine. The sword didn't want her to *kick* people. It wanted to cut. It thirsted for contact with matter.

Now that she was on her feet, Connor turned his cloaker back on. The last soldier was twirling in panic, trying to find an enemy to attack. Ellis sliced his gun through the stock and drove a knee into his stomach before the useless barrel clattered onto the concrete floor. As he moaned, an invisible hand yanked the soldier's helmet off, and a dart appeared in his neck.

The blood drained from Ellis' face as her father popped into the envelope of her cloaker, and she looked over his shoulder. She couldn't bear to look at his face, and she *really* couldn't bear to look at the floor. She didn't have to look to understand what she had done. Her boots slipped in the blood as she pulled Connor toward the elevator.

"The lightsilk..." he protested. She raised the blade and slashed the glittering net. The fabric fluttered away from the frame, and Ellis leapt over the tattered remains.

Connor joined her at the elevator. "We can't take this. They'll be waiting for us."

"I wasn't planning a direct route," Ellis told him grimly and cut through the thick steel like it was cotton candy, then drew her sword in a wide circle. When she was done, she kicked the metal in with her feet. Before she stepped into the elevator shaft, she replaced the blade in its scabbard and slung the whole thing over her shoulder.

"Are you all right?" Connor asked, searching her face. His eyes bored into her, and Ellis shook her head. They couldn't afford to stop and try to understand what was happening. They had to keep moving.

There were metal pegs on the wall to give the maintenance workers access to the shaft. With their assistance, Ellis flew up the wall, allowing herself to think about Charlie for the first time. Prison bars couldn't stop her. The guards couldn't either. Nothing could, now that she had the sword.

The levels were unmarked, but Ellis made a guess based on the distance they'd traveled. She was about to unsheathe the shadow blade when Connor shouted for her to stop. He pointed at an emergency door release on the side of the shaft. The sword shivered with disappointment as she dropped the hilt and pulled the release.

The elevator doors opened into a small airlock. Ellis touched the hilt of the sword again, sure this was her chance, but Connor stopped her again and held up a key card. He'd taken it off the guard she'd killed. Ellis, who hadn't seen him take it, looked away from the blood on the photograph of a grim-faced man with close-cropped hair and blue eyes.

CHAPTER TWENTY-TWO

The key card got them through the airlock and into the hallway beyond, but moments later, someone came to investigate. "Why the *fuck* aren't you answering your radio, Corp—"

The soldier marching down the hall stopped dead when he saw the empty airlock. The German Shepherd padding beside him did not. The dog surged to where Connor and Ellis were hiding, pinning them against the wall in a riot of high-decibel barking. Ellis took a deep breath. If it didn't eat their faces, the dog might be able to help them.

The soldier stared at the spot, trying to figure out what had set the German Shepherd off. Then the dog stopped. It whined, then wagged its tail and padded back to its handler's side. There, it sat on its haunches and winked at her.

Ellis thought that was what had happened, but she wasn't a hundred percent sure. The expression in the dog's eyes reminded her of Flower. After a pause, the dog spun and barked at the far wall, drawing its handler's attention away from Ellis and her father.

The soldier turned with the dog. "What is *up* with you, Ivan? Make up your mind, boy," he muttered. As he reached for something at his belt, Connor shot a dart into his exposed neck. The soldier slumped to the floor.

Ivan rushed over and licked his handler's face, then whined, then looked at Ellis with confusion in his eyes. Apparently, the cloakers didn't block smells.

Ellis took a chance and flicked hers off. Raising her hands above her head, she clapped three times. Ivan cocked his head, whined, and licked his handler's face again.

"He's okay, boy. He's just taking a nap."

Gingerly, Ellis stretched out a hand and scratched behind the dog's ears. His tail wagged, and she knew she was in.

"Do you know where Percy is?" Ellis asked. "Percy? Small guy? Loves to chat. Usually wears really atrocious shirts, but probably not down here." The tail wagged harder. Ellis unclipped the lead from the dog's neck. "Go on, boy. Take us to your leader."

Ivan trotted down the hall.

"You think the dog knows where they are?" Connor asked.

Ellis flicked her cloaker back on. "Yes. I do. He has that look in his eyes that Percy's animals get. I'd bet a gold bar that dog knows what's going on."

Connor nodded, and they followed the wagging tail. Unlike the vault below, Level Three was segmented into ordinary rooms and corridors. Ellis unsheathed her sword and held it in front of her as they walked, trying to look at the blade. It continued to slide away from her.

"I don't like that thing," Connor remarked as they rounded a corner. The hilt jerked resentfully in response, which didn't brighten Connor's frown.

Static blurped behind them, and there was noise from the corridor ahead. A man was screaming. Ellis' adrenaline spiked as she saw familiar-looking slots in the heavy doors lining one wall of a corridor. Just the right size for a food tray. They had reached the containment cells.

There was another scream. Ivan trotted over and sat down outside one of the doors, staring warily through the food slot. It flapped open in time with the frantic cries for help. As Ellis drew closer, she could understand the message, and her heart sank.

The man inside wasn't Charlie or Percy.

"You fucked up the lightsilk nets. Supposed to be equipped for MECs, but… Lockdown… Fuck… Is that Ivan?"

There were two men arguing inside the cell. They weren't prisoners, or they hadn't been until recently. They were guards who'd been thrown into a cell. She could tell from their clothing.

"Ivan. Go get help," one said.

"It's no fucking use, Bugs. The dog went spooky."

Taking a deep breath, Ellis turned off the cloaker and stepped into view of the food slot. "Hello?" The slot slammed closed, and there were rustles inside the cell.

Then someone called, "Help. Open the door!"

"I don't think so," Ellis said. "What's going on? Where are Charlie and Percy?"

Silence. Ellis tried again, but no one responded. The prisoners whispered conspiratorially.

Ellis *could* slice open the door, grab the men by the necks, and demand answers as they cowered beneath her blade. It would feel very good to release her anger. The ring on her finger shivered, and the sword emitted an encouraging pulse. Ellis ignored them and turned to her father. "Sebastian and the others came through here. Where'd they go?"

"Maybe they returned to the storage bay and escaped back into the tunnel."

"We might as well move in that direction."

As they walked, Connor cleared his throat. "It was unwise to show yourself to those soldiers. They could report our presence to their superiors."

The shadow sword's hilt vibrated. It was *laughing* at Connor's comment, thirsty for blood and rejoicing at the thought of conflict.

"I could go back and cut their heads off," Ellis offered. Connor looked uncertain, unable to tell if she was joking. Ellis wasn't sure either. The sword wanted violence, but surely, it wouldn't stoop to decapitating captive soldiers. Ellis tried and failed to look at the blade again.

There were more lightsilk nets in these corridors, and Ellis cut through them, relishing the feeling of the blade slicing through the air.

Ivan led them toward the storeroom through which the other team had entered the level. The halls were silent, and when they reached a set of double doors, the dog paused. He quirked his head as if he were listening to a voice inside the room, then sat on his haunches. When Ellis approached, the dog barked, teeth gleaming white over a dripping red tongue. She stepped closer, and the dog growled.

Percy's animals weren't normally violent. Ivan's behavior meant that he was either no longer in contact with Percy…or he was warning her.

The dog whined. "Are you warning me, buddy?" Ellis asked.

Ivan's head tilted again, and he barked once.

She would have bet anything that Percy was behind those doors. Why was he warning her? "Percy is trying to talk to us," she whispered to her father. "Something's wrong."

"Should we retreat?" Connor asked.

"There's no time. I think they're all behind that door."

After telling Ivan to stay, she moved to the end of the hall and put her left palm on the wall.

"What are you doing?" Connor asked.

"Surprising them. Are you ready?" Ellis replied. Her face was flushed, and beads of sweat stood out on her skin.

When her father nodded uncertainly, Ellis sliced a waist-high hole in the wall. Her own personal doggy door.

Whoever Percy wanted her to be afraid of would probably only guard the door. That was what Ellis would do. Her best hope of getting control of the situation was taking the enemy by surprise. Reluctantly, she replaced the sword in its scabbard.

It didn't want to go, so she had to shove it down by force before slinging it over her shoulder. Then she dove through the hole she'd cut and crawled along the edge of the storage bay on her hands and knees. She counted on her cloaker to keep her concealed.

"Did you hear that?" someone asked, too far in the distance for Ellis to make out the speaker's identity. She SEAL-crawled forward on her elbows, approaching the noise.

"Dog..."

Ivan was barking outside the door again, which drew their attention off her. *Smart dog.* Moving between two metal racks, she sat up and peered at the far wall.

Charlie. Ellis' heart soared at the sight of his face, and she let out a cry of joy before double-checking that her hush puppy was activated. It was, so she whooped in delight. He awkwardly scratched his nose with his shoulder. He was sitting cross-legged on the floor with his hands behind his back. Handcuffed, she guessed. Ellis frowned. Had he and the others escaped but been recaptured?

When Ellis edged forward to get a better view, she saw that Percy was seated next to Charlie in a similar position. A single standing figure guarded both of them. When Ellis sat up to get a better look, the person spun.

It was Ollie, scanning the room with the purple-tinted glasses that allowed him to see shadow magic.

"Ollie." Ellis sighed in relief. Ollie couldn't hear her, so she flicked her cloaker and hush puppy off.

Ollie raised his gun and shook his head. "Stop right there." Rami was at his back, ready with a dart gun.

"Ollie, Rami, it's me," Ellis repeated stupidly. Something was wrong.

When Percy and Charlie saw her, pain spread across their faces.

"Ellis! Don't—" Percy shouted. Before he could finish his sentence, the butt of a rifle came down on his head. His scream cut off when Sebastian activated a hush puppy and tossed it between Charlie and Percy. They soundlessly yelled in her direction. Behind them, Mikhail and Rose sat up with panicked expressions.

Sebastian had clearly changed the plan. He eyed Ellis, and his gaze alighted on the sword slung over her shoulder. "Hand it over."

Ollie's gun twitched. Ellis thought he was going to lower it, but the barrel turned toward Charlie's head. His mouth closed.

"No," Ellis whispered. "You can't hurt him. I won't let you."

"Do as the captain says," Ollie ordered. His hands were shaking.

"I'm in charge of this mission," Ellis stammered, though she understood that the situation had galloped out of her grasp.

"The sword, Ellis," Sebastian snapped, his fury growing.

"You were always going to betray me," Ellis realized.

"You want your little friends. I want the sword," Sebastian explained. "We're both going to get what we want."

Ellis suddenly realized what was missing from the picture. "Where are Landon and Ilva and Trissa?"

"They're alive. That's all you need to know for now."

Ellis heard a low growl at her back. She thought Ivan had followed them inside, but when she turned, she realized her father had made the noise.

Ellis looked for Jerel, but he wasn't with his *Violet Eel*

crewmates. He must have stayed with the others. *At least they have a medic.* "Are they okay?"

"Give me the sword, and I'll tell you." Sebastian didn't look well.

"They're fine," Rami told her. Sebastian gritted his teeth.

Ellis locked eyes with Charlie. She was relieved to see him after all this time. He was unshaven and tired, but he smiled when she looked at him.

"Are you going to hand it over now or after I shoot one of your friends?" Sebastian asked.

Ellis shrugged the scabbard off her shoulder. The sword maintained its psychic pull, but it ebbed when she tugged the ring off. She had feared she might not be able to let go, but the metal slid off easily, warming as it left her finger.

"Get the sword, Rami," Sebastian's voice was clipped, curtness disguising a deeper emotion. He might be dying of hunger, but he wanted someone else to taste the food for poison.

"You're afraid," Ellis mused. "You think the sword's going to hurt you, so you're going to throw Rami under the bus."

Sebastian's eyes blazed with anger as the words hit their target. Ellis had seen him for who he really was, and he was furious. He hadn't been able to use the ring, and he was afraid that he couldn't handle the sword.

"I thought we were friends," Ellis commented as the chef stepped forward. "You made me waffles."

Rami looked sad and a little embarrassed. "I'm a company man. Sebastian gave me a good life. I'm just following orders."

"The sword is going to kill you," Ellis whispered. Her

hand shook as she held out the scabbard. She didn't know what would happen if the wrong person touched the black metal, but she doubted it would be good.

"Don't worry about me." Rami struggled to maintain a casual tone as he took the ring from Ellis' hand and slid it onto his finger. "Think of how quickly I'll be able to chop vegetables after I get my hands on this bad boy."

He wrapped his fingers around the hilt and grabbed the scabbard with his other hand. When he slid the blade out a few inches, Sebastian sucked in his breath, eyes plastered to the abyssal darkness of the edge.

"Go on," Sebastian urged. "Take it out."

Rami was unable to speak. When Ellis looked at his face, she gasped. The chef's easy smile was gone, replaced by teeth bared in pain. Terror had seized his body, and his attention was fixed on his right hand.

It was frozen to the hilt. His white fingers were lifeless, and his marine-blue skin faded to powdery gray as Ellis watched.

"Let go of the sword!" she shouted. *Give it back. I want it back.*

Rami's terrified eyes widened. He couldn't let go, given that his fingers were frozen to the hilt. The skin discoloration was traveling toward his elbow at a dangerous rate. Stepping forward, she grabbed the sword and tried to pry it out of Rami's fingers. He screamed in pain, and she let go when she heard a crunch. The tip of Rami's pinkie had crumbled like one of his freeze-dried strawberries. The part of her that missed the sword thought, *It serves him right.*

The thought made the rest of Ellis want to vomit. She

had to help him, but she didn't know what was happening. *I never should have let go of the sword.*

Stepping out from behind her, Connor raised one hand and spun a skein of shadow magic into a blade. In a single swift movement, he sliced through Rami's arm just below the elbow.

Ellis surged forward as the shadow sword fell and caught it by the scabbard. Rami's hand was still frozen to the hilt. As she looked on in horror, it crumbled to dust that rained onto the concrete floor around the black pearl ring.

With a cry of surprise, Ellis re-sheathed the blade and clutched the scabbard to her breast. *I'll never let anyone take it again.* Reaching down, she plucked the ring from the dust. Without thinking, she slipped it back on her finger, relieved by the cold touch of the black metal.

Rami stared at the bleeding stump of his arm as the color drained from his face. His eyes met Ellis', and then Connor blocked her view as he rushed to provide first aid. Fabric ripped and a bandage appeared, and Connor secured a temporary tourniquet around Rami's arm.

Ellis turned to Sebastian, face flushing. "Are you going to take us to Jerel now? Rami needs a medic."

"He's up in the tunnel," Sebastian told her after a moment. The captain's grasp on the situation had slipped, his horror at the emergency amputation straining his resolve. "They're all in the staging area." He was unable to look his injured cook in the eyes. The gun dropped to his side. "Come on."

"No." Ellis shook her head. "You wanted the sword. I think you should take it."

She held out the scabbard, but she knew he wouldn't touch it. Sebastian shivered, staring at his reflection in the shining black metal.

"Go on," she urged. "Isn't this what you've been dreaming about? The ultimate weapon? Some protection it offered you." She looked pointedly at Rami.

"I'm sorry," Sebastian stammered. Dropping his gun, he moved to the corner of the room on autopilot, flinging aside the shelves they'd pulled across the tunnel entrance. Ellis stayed with Ollie, her father, Rami, and the four dazed hostages.

"Put that thing down," Ellis shouted at Ollie, pointing at his gun with the scabbard. The chain of command had fallen apart, and he looked like he was about to follow in its footsteps. After a moment, he lowered the gun.

"Thanks," Charlie grinned. "I appreciate it." Ellis favored him with a wide smile.

"Take him to Jerel," she told Connor, nodding at the tunnel. Her father swiftly guided Rami away. Metal clattered as they disappeared.

"Go with them," Ellis told Ollie. She didn't know if it was her or the sword, but he obeyed.

The hostages looked stupefied. Ellis slung the shadow sword over her shoulder, plucked the hush puppy from the floor near Charlie's feet, and flicked it off. Despite that, everyone stayed silent.

"Ellis Burton! My favorite sexy vigilante!" Mikhail exclaimed. "I had hoped to say this under more pleasant circumstances, but will you remove my handcuffs now?" He turned around, and Ellis laughed. Charlie looked like he wanted to kill the young Russian. Ellis dissolved Mikhail's handcuffs, then did the same for Rose and Percy.

Finally, she turned to Charlie. When his hands popped free, Ellis wrapped him in her arms. "You're not dead!" She ran her hands through his hair, and they came away greasy. *How romantic.*

"Trissa didn't tell you?" Charlie asked, voice muffled. He stretched, wincing as feeling returned to his arms. He was drawn and exhausted, but she took comfort from the warmth in his eyes.

"I eventually learned the truth. A lot has happened. There were complications."

"We've been a mite busy ourselves," Percy interjected cheerfully.

Nails clicked on the concrete. Ellis dropped into a defensive crouch, ready to face a new enemy. It was Ivan, who had apparently gotten the go-ahead from Percy to join the party. The dog licked Percy's face, and the two had a silent tete-a-tete.

"I'm still not sure what's happening," Charlie muttered. Now that she had some breathing room, she noticed thin red lines crisscrossing his face. Lightsilk burns. No wonder he hadn't undone his handcuffs.

"Those *bastards*!" Ellis gently touched his face. Closing her eyes, she sent a burst of healing magic into his skin. After a moment, the red welts looked less angry.

"Ellis!" Charlie exclaimed, amazed.

"What?"

"Your shadow magic. It's back!"

"Like I said, Trissa and I found each other eventually.

She and my father perfected the formula." Ellis grinned, tapping the bottle of shadow magic potion at her waist.

He pulled her into a hug, which Ellis didn't resist. "How's *your* shadow magic?" she finally asked.

"Useless at the moment," Charlie growled. "Fucking lightsilk."

"Don't I know it." Ellis sighed.

It was going to be a long climb out. Climbing down had been difficult for some of their party, even the ones with drow superstrength. Getting four humans in bad shape up a steep rock shaft would be something else entirely, and the dog wouldn't be able to make it.

"You have to leave him here," Ellis told Percy. "It won't be safe."

Percy sighed as he scratched the dog's back. "I suppose you're right. Well, boy, you've got my thanks. You know how to get in touch if you ever need me."

Ivan woofed, looking distraught.

Percy's somber expression brightened when Rose put an arm around his shoulder. She was half a head taller than he was, so she had to lean down to whisper into his ear. Whatever she said, it cheered him up. "What's this I hear about a tunnel? I thought we were going to have to fight our way out."

"Nope." Ellis led them toward the staging area.

The trip back to the surface was as hard as she'd feared. After they were all in the staging area, Connor collapsed the stretch of tunnel that led to the storage area. That would keep the military busy for quite a while.

After that, it was mostly a question of brute effort. Charlie and the others hadn't gotten much exercise during their confinement. They didn't complain, but Ellis saw that they were struggling. Particularly Percy, who was older and had never been very athletic. He stayed next to Rose, and they helped one another through the tough spots.

Jerel did his best for Rami's injury. He administered a rustcap potion to replenish the drow's blood volume and loaded him up with painkillers. Ollie attached himself to the medic, happy to have someone familiar giving him orders.

Ilva wanted to kill Sebastian, and Sebastian seemed inclined to let her try. However, cooler heads prevailed. Connor separated them and sent Ilva to Ellis, who had taken up the rear guard. Charlie stayed with her.

As she climbed, her fingers danced over the scabbard of the shadow sword. It had been stupid for Sebastian to try to take it from her. It was all hers. She enjoyed the frisson of energy between the cold ring on her finger and the sword's hilt.

Charlie seemed concerned about it, and there wasn't much she could say to comfort him. "We only found you because of the sword." She filled Charlie in on the coup at the Homestead and her work with the *Violet Eel*. She asked him about his imprisonment, but he was too out of breath to give her much information.

They progressed a hundred feet, then five hundred, then a thousand. Finally, daylight filtered into the tunnel. The last leg was the hardest. When Ellis pulled herself up the final few handholds into a decrepit wooden cabin, no one welcomed her. They were all stretched out on the splintery floor, panting with exhaustion.

The strike team had dug the tunnel's entrance inside an

old mining shack. They'd hoped the rickety structure would conceal their presence, and as far as Ellis could tell, it had worked. She was drenched with sweat in seconds, the hot desert sun boiling away the lingering underground chill. Ellis let herself lay on the floor for a few minutes, luxuriating in the cold air wafting off the shadow sword. Then, she dragged herself to her feet to locate their cache of water.

Sebastian was sitting in the other room with a half-full water jug on his lap. As Ellis approached him, he upended it on his head.

"You should drink that, not bathe in it," Ellis remarked.

Sebastian ran a hand through his wet hair, ignoring her. Ellis decided to take her own advice and unscrewed the lid of another jug. The water was warm and unsatisfying. They *really* had to get out of here. "*Fifteen minutes. Then we move out!* The military is almost certainly looking for us already. We can't afford to stop moving."

Sebastian nodded but grabbed the leg of her pants when she turned to leave. "I'm sorry. The sword was a mistake. I shouldn't have tried to take it."

"You should apologize to Rami, not me." There was a cold edge in her voice that she barely recognized. *Is that the sword talking?*

"I will. First thing. I promise." He gulped more water. "What are you going to do now?"

Ellis ran her hand over the hilt of the sword. "I don't know." Returning to the Homestead might be impossible, and the Outpost was gone.

"Will you come back to the *Eel* with me?" Sebastian asked. He sounded pathetic.

"You held my friends hostage," Ellis growled. "I finally got Ch…got all my friends back, and then you pointed a gun at them."

Sebastian's eyes were glued to the shadow sword in Ellis' hands. He edged away from her when she stepped closer. "Let's just say I learned my lesson. Rami's stable, by the way. Jerel took him out to the van."

"I want you to understand something." Sweat dripped off Ellis' hands and froze when the droplets hit the scabbard. She gripped the hilt. "If you ever threaten my friends or family again, I will kill you, and I will slice the *Violet Eel* in half."

He nodded miserably.

"I *will* consider working with you in the future under one condition."

"What's that?"

"I want you to wait a month before you announce the existence of the drow. Use that time to think about what you're doing, considering we might have just started a war with the military."

As if the sky had heard her, a plane zoomed overhead. A surveillance drone? Maybe not. "Like I said, we should go."

"Okay," Sebastian agreed. Ellis offered him a hand, but he waved it away. "No, not that. I need another minute. What you said about waiting? I agree. If you come back with us, I will wait a month before I do anything. If you're willing, we can try to get a handle on what the hell that sword is. Maybe it was a mistake to look for it."

The sword jerked, insulted. Sebastian saw the movement and went pale.

"Deal." Ellis didn't want to talk about the sword

anymore. She held out her hand, but when Sebastian took it, they were both so sweaty that it was difficult to retain a grip. Somehow, they managed, and she pulled him to his feet, then went to find her family. They were huddled in a tight knot near the van, and they weren't thrilled when she told them she was returning to the ship.

"Sebastian is fickle and untrustworthy," Ilva snapped.

"He's scared," Ellis countered.

Ilva snorted. "That's worse."

"It's not just that," Ellis continued. "The sword has a pull. I feel it, and I think it affected him." It was affecting her now in ways she didn't understand. She put her face against the cold metal of the scabbard. It was useful as a portable A/C unit. Too bad it was a cursed artifact.

"We don't have to stay on the *Violet Eel* forever, but we need backup for now, and I'm not sure we can get it at the Homestead. I think the ship is the best of a bunch of bad options."

Sebastian came over. "You should turn your cloakers on. We need to load the van. Please," he added after a minute.

Ilva separated from the group and walked toward him, then leaned close. "You claim to be a captain."

He nodded. "I don't *claim* it. It's a fact."

"Hm. In that case, I require a service from you, *Captain,*" Ilva's voice dripped disdain.

"What might that be?" Sebastian asked.

Ilva smiled. "I believe it is a human naval tradition. I need you to perform a wedding."

Ellis gaped. Leaning against a rickety wooden wall in exhaustion, Connor smiled faintly. "How interesting. Did you rekindle an old romance while we were separated at the Homestead?"

Ilva glared at him. "I decided to accept your proposal."

"Get your butts in the van, and I'll marry you to anyone you want." Sebastian sounded miserable.

Ellis had mixed feelings about the development. Ilva had not been a warm presence during her childhood. Sometimes, she'd been downright cruel, but they had come to understand one another. Ellis understood her father better now, too.

Ellis went over and wrapped her arms around both of them. "I can't wait. Right now, let's get back to the boat."

THE STORY CONTINUES

The story continues with The Chronicles of Shadow Bourne book eight, coming soon to Amazon and Kindle Unlimited.

A dark sword. An ancient monster. One hero caught between two worlds. Can the Drow fulfill her destiny?

Ellis never asked to be humanity's last hope. But with a supernatural creature ravaging Los Angeles and the military closing in on her people, she has no choice.

As chaos engulfs the city, Ellis must master her mysterious shadow sword and uncover its connection to the rampaging monster. With her father, Connor and boyfriend, Charlie by her side, the Drow is going deeper into a hidden realm of old magic and long-buried secrets.

Will everyone come out alive?

Time is running out. The monster is growing stronger, and too many lives hang in the balance. To save everyone Ellis has vowed to protect, she must confront the beast and the painful history it represents.

Can Ellis bridge two worlds and bring peace, or will ancient grudges destroy everything? Will her forbidden love with Charlie survive the coming storm?

Find out now! Scroll up and buy Drow Requiem to see where adventure takes Ellis next.

Get sneak peeks, exclusive giveaways, behind the scenes content, and more. PLUS you'll be notified of special **one day only fan pricing** on new releases.

Sign up today to get free stories.

Visit: https://marthacarr.com/read-free-stories/

AUTHOR NOTES: MARTHA CARR

WRITTEN JULY 23, 2024

I've started a project answering questions for my son about my life. I realized after last year's fifth round of cancer, and then chemo this time that he was expecting me to die sooner rather than later. It's been a lot for him to deal with and there isn't much I can do to make it better, except tell him stories that I can leave behind – eventually. Hopefully, a long time from now. I'm going to let you guys listen in as well.

My author notes right now are going to be answers to questions and all of you can get to know me better, too. Maybe inspire, maybe give you a laugh along the way.

Today's question is: If this was the last thing I wrote, what words of wisdom would I share?

That's a doozy of a question given why I started this project in the first place. At least I've had some solid practice thinking about it and probably sharing it as well.

It's a great idea to really set aside all the daily or even monthly and yearly worries that nag at the brain. Will it rain enough this summer? What will I get my sister for

Christmas? Did I pay that phone bill yet? I need to lose those few pounds. Does that tooth hurt? There are hundreds of them floating in an out all day long. Most go unnoticed or noticed for only a moment but they still add to the background noise.

Well, fourteen years ago I got a break from the noise when a callous surgeon surprised me, with you sitting by my side at only 21 years old, and flipped through a notebook of gruesome color pictures of what the last year of my life was going to look like. No warning at all. He announced without any lead in that I had a one percent chance of lasting more than a year. It felt like he was throwing me a bone.

Moments after the notebook was closed and taken away, he asked if I had any questions. All I could do was glance at you sitting next to me and wonder what it was doing to you. There wasn't a chance I was going to ask this man, who lacked compassion on a grand scale, anything at all in front of you. God knows what he would have shared.

At that point, my hands were shaking like I was a piano wire someone had plucked. Mostly, I was worried about you.

But when we left the little room, the surgeon already on to someone else (he didn't wait around to comfort or say words of encouragement, which was probably best), you looked at me and said with conviction, "Weren't you listening. He said there was hope. I remember feeling like most of the tension drained out of me because I thought, if you heard hope in that room, you'd be okay.

Then, for the next few months, I lived in this strange middle ground of being in this world and wondering if I was on my way out. I remember Christmas was a few months away and people were talking about their plans and I didn't feel attached to the conversation at all. The biggest surprise was how peaceful I felt. I had a much better perspective on all the things I worried about all the time. None of them mattered. I could see that they really didn't influence my quality of life and they would all work out one way or another, some better than others. All the striving and people pleasing and trying to control outcome melted away. For once, I knew what it really felt like to live in the moment, and without that background noise.

Of course, I didn't die and slowly over time my odds went up, mysteriously. They still can't say why although there are theories. Whatever, I'm here, that's what counts. And I had a feeling that as my odds of living rose, I would take back those worries. I didn't want to but it was kind of inevitable, being human and all.

However, getting older kind of gives me a second chance that's a bit gentler. My expiration date isn't so firmly stamped on my forehead. This is what I would want to say to you if I knew this was my last message. I love you, just as you are, right in this moment. I don't need to know all the details of what's going right or what's going wrong to feel that way. I just do because I'm your Mom and I believe in you. I'm all in on you, and I hope I've learned to do the same for myself as well.

All the fancy trappings are so much fun and I love me a good bougie time, but what has mattered most is watching you be happy in the moment, and feeling happiness for myself in the same way, for no good reason. I still forget that that's possible from time to time and I have to reset back to it, but I've never forgotten that lesson. Oh, and side note, when delivering really hard news, slow down and show compassion and take your time. Love you. Love, Mom. More adventures (and years) to follow.

AUTHOR NOTES: MICHAEL ANDERLE

WRITTEN JULY 8, 2024

First off, thank you for not only diving into this story but also sticking around to read these author notes tucked away at the back. I appreciate you letting me bend your ear for a bit!

Living with a Legal Eagle: The Joys and Challenges of a Lawyer-after-University

So, here's a fun fact that some of you might know, but others probably don't: my better half is a juris doctorate in law. Now, you'd think having a legal expert in the house would be all sunshine and rainbows, right?

Well, let me tell you, it's been... *interesting*.

Don't get me wrong, it's been incredibly helpful in business. But in our personal life? Let's just say it's added some unexpected twists and turns.

You see, the way lawyers are taught to think can strike at odd times, kind of like a cat deciding to zoom around the house at 3 AM for no apparent reason. Furthermore, the way lawyers think can often be at odds with a creative who doesn't explain himself…uh, or herself… very well.

Now, imagine: You're having a perfectly normal conversation, and suddenly, WHAM!

The significant others legal brain kicks in.

Here are five times when living with a lawyer-in-training can make you feel like you've stepped into an episode of Law & Order (these may, or may not, have ANY relationship to reality. They are just examples, please do not take them as real…like ever):

1. **The Great Pizza Debate:** You suggest ordering pizza for dinner. Simple, right? Not necessrily. Suddenly, you're knee-deep in a discussion about the potential liabilities of delivery drivers and the legal implications of tipping. By the time you've reached a verdict, the pizza place is closed or you have decided to make some soup out of a package.
2. **The Case of the Missing Socks:** You casually mention that you can't find your favorite pair of socks. Next thing you know, you're being cross-examined about your laundry habits, the last known whereabouts of said socks, and whether you have any alibi for the time they went missing. (This example hits way too close to reality for many of you who live with legal-eagles, I'm sure.)
3. **The Parking Ticket Saga:** You get a parking ticket and want to vent. Instead, you end up with a full breakdown of parking law, a dissection of

the ticket's validity, and a strategy for contesting it that would make Perry Mason proud. I've lived the contesting it part (I didn't get the ticket, Judith did. The story is infamous when she went to contest it on a dark and stormy night.)

4. **The Great TV Remote Custody Battle:** Deciding what to watch on TV becomes a negotiation worthy of international peace talks. Terms are defined, precedents are cited, and by the time you've reached an agreement, you're both too tired to watch anything. (This doesn't happen so much in my house. I read books. Judith watches TV. When Judith wants me to watch TV with her, she has learned to use her other degree in International Marketing to inform me why I'm going to like this.)
5. **The Birthday Gift Clause:** You're about to buy a birthday gift when suddenly you're hit with questions about gift tax implications, the legal definition of a gift, and whether accepting said gift constitutes a verbal contract. Who knew gift-giving could be so complicated? (Note – this is a big deal if the birthday gift is for someone that you also do business with, just saying.)

There you have it! A few ways that life can get a bit screwy when your spouse has been trained to think legally. It's like living with a walking, talking fine print disclaimer.

A real downer for a creative who loves to bend rules he didn't even realize were rules with ramifications.

But you know what? Despite the occasional impromptu

legal lecture or surprise cross-examination over lunch, I wouldn't have it any other way. This is what I tell myself, anyway.

Until next time, may your conversations be free of legal jargon and your socks always be found in pairs.

Ad Aeternitatem,
Michael Anderle

P.S. For more musings, sneak peeks, and the occasional legal anecdote, don't forget to subscribe to my newsletter: MORE STORIES with Michael. Check it out here: https://michael.beehiiv.com/

BOOKS BY MARTHA CARR

Other Series in the Oriceran Universe:

THE LEIRA CHRONICLES

CASE FILES OF AN URBAN WITCH

SOUL STONE MAGE

THE KACY CHRONICLES

MIDWEST MAGIC CHRONICLES

THE FAIRHAVEN CHRONICLES

I FEAR NO EVIL

THE DANIEL CODEX SERIES

SCHOOL OF NECESSARY MAGIC

SCHOOL OF NECESSARY MAGIC: RAINE CAMPBELL

ALISON BROWNSTONE

FEDERAL AGENTS OF MAGIC

SCIONS OF MAGIC

THE UNBELIEVABLE MR. BROWNSTONE

DWARF BOUNTY HUNTER

ACADEMY OF NECESSARY MAGIC

MAGIC CITY CHRONICLES

ROGUE AGENTS OF MAGIC

OTHER BOOKS BY JUDITH BERENS

OTHER BOOKS BY MARTHA CARR

JOIN THE ORICERAN UNIVERSE FAN GROUP ON FACEBOOK!

BOOKS BY MICHAEL ANDERLE

Sign up for the LMBPN email list to be notified of new releases and special deals!

https://lmbpn.com/email/

For a complete list of books by Michael Anderle, please visit:

www.lmbpn.com/ma-books/

CONNECT WITH THE AUTHORS

Martha Carr Social

Website: http://www.marthacarr.com

Facebook: https://www.facebook.com/groups/MarthaCarrFans/

Michael Anderle Social

Website: http://lmbpn.com

Email List: https://michael.beehiiv.com/

https://www.facebook.com/LMBPNPublishing

https://twitter.com/MichaelAnderle

https://www.instagram.com/lmbpn_publishing/

https://www.bookbub.com/authors/michael-anderle

www.ingramcontent.com/pod-product-compliance
Lightning Source LLC
LaVergne TN
LVHW041912070526
838199LV00051BA/2595
9798888789919